De~

I had the honor of writing both the ~~~ ~~ ~~~t books in the original MAITLAND MATERNITY series. While working on them, I got to know various members of the family pretty well and saying goodbye wasn't easy. It never is for me, which is why I tend to revisit towns and families I've created. So when Silhouette Romance asked if I'd be interested in working on another MAITLAND MATERNITY story, I jumped at the chance. It allowed me the opportunity to get back with Megan Maitland, one of my favorite characters, and her family. And also to create new characters, as well. Working on *The Inheritance* also represented a new first for me. Despite all the books I've been fortunate enough to write, I've never touched on the subject of the older woman, younger man relationship. The pairing is getting more and more common these days, but for me, it was new territory to explore. So, for me, working on this book involved something old and something new. All we need is to borrow something blue and we're all set for another Maitland wedding. Did you ever doubt it would happen? As always, I thank you for reading one of my stories, and from the bottom of my heart I wish you happiness and love.

Love,

Marie

Maitland
Maternity THE
INHERITANCE

Marie Ferrarella

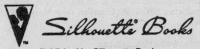

Silhouette Books

Published by Silhouette Books
America's Publisher of Contemporary Romance

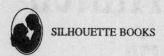

SILHOUETTE BOOKS

THE INHERITANCE

Copyright © 2001 by Marie Rydzynski-Ferrarella

ISBN 0-373-48453-4

Visit Silhouette at www.eHarlequin.com

Printed in U.S.A.

To Patricia Smith
My Brand-New Guardian Angel
Here's to a Long "Guardianship"
With Love
Marie

Chapter 1

The last thing Rafe Maitland wanted to see at the end of a long, hard day, spent mostly in the saddle overseeing the hundred and one things that went into running a smooth ranching operation for his boss, was a prim, proper-looking woman standing in front of his door wearing a slate-gray suit, sensible shoes and oversize glasses.

His annoyed gaze swept quickly over her. The woman was clutching some kind of briefcase.

Saleswoman?

As he walked toward her, feeling every one of the twelve hours he'd put in since before dawn, the ends of his temper unraveled a little more with each step he took. Never one to run off at the mouth, he was feeling even more uncommunicative than usual. He just wanted a long, hot shower and some time to himself before the evening had a chance to unfold in front of him. Half an hour by himself. Was that too much to ask?

Apparently so.

The woman looked like someone's timid maiden aunt, right down to her brown hair, which was pulled back in what, in his book, amounted to a no-nonsense hairdo. A woman's hair should be soft, flowing, Rafe thought critically. Tempting a man to run his fingers through it, not silently ordering "hands off."

Who was she and what the hell was she doing here in the middle of almost nowhere?

If he'd had put in an order for a woman on his doorstep, it would have been the vibrant, curvaceous type. And soft, the kind of soft that made a man's mouth water, not the kind of soft that indicated an untoned body.

Not that he had the energy for the former type of woman these days, he thought. Not with the hours he was putting in on what amounted to next to no sleep. He figured the sleep would come once he got used to being a substitute parent. And Bethany finally got used to having him around and stopped calling out for her parents.

That was the worst of it, hearing her crying the baby words in the middle of the night and knowing that when he appeared, it wouldn't cause her to stop, to smile the way she had when either Lil or Rory had come to scoop her out of her crib. He was just her godfather, not her parent. But he intended to be much more. All he needed was a little time. And luck.

Rafe swallowed the weary, sad sigh that materialized out of nowhere before it had a chance to escape. He didn't allow himself to display signs of weakness—even if he was ready to drop in his tracks.

His eyes narrowed as he arrived at his doorstep. The woman looked as if she wanted to flinch but was struggling not to. What was that about? Mentally, he shrugged away the stray bit of curiosity.

Nope, he certainly had enough on his plate without having to put up with any sort of an intrusion. Seeing her open her mouth, he stopped her before she could launch into some kind of a sales pitch.

"Sorry if they misdirected you at the main house, ma'am, but whatever you're selling, I'm not buying, so you might as well leave."

Greer Lawford gripped the handle of the leather briefcase she was holding in both hands a little more tightly as the word went through her. *Ma'am.* The polite address made her wince inwardly. It also made her feel a thousand years old instead of thirty and a great deal older than this handsome, rugged-looking cowboy standing in front of her. She was hot, somewhat irritable even though she was at the tail end of the long trip she'd been on since yesterday morning and, quite honestly, more than a little tense. She had no intention of being cavalierly dismissed, or even of accepting no for an answer.

Greer was, quite simply, on a mission. Sent by her employer, Megan Maitland, she had been told to do whatever it took to lure this somewhat larger-than-life specimen of manhood to Austin, Texas, and keep him there as the rest of the clan gathered together for what promised to be a huge family celebration.

And whatever Megan Maitland wanted, the matriarch of the Maitland family was accustomed to getting. Not because she was pandered to, or because of any supposed divine right of the moneyed class, but because Megan Maitland's heart was always behind her requests and everyone took pleasure in making her happy. Greer was no exception.

That this latest request involved gathering together all the heretofore unknown factions of the Maitland clan under one large roof at one time just made Greer that much more determined to see it happen. She'd never had a family and felt she could be forgiven if she acted as though the Maitland family were her own. She had dutifully sent out all the invitations, but when Robert Maitland's estranged branch of the family had not responded, she'd taken it upon herself to ferret them out even before Mrs. Maitland had said anything. She saw it as a challenge. Rafe Maitland, the youngest, had been her first target.

She felt her palms grow just the slightest bit damp. This was about Christmas, she told herself, the time for peace and goodwill toward men. Even somewhat hostile ones like this one appeared to be.

"I'm not selling anything," she told him firmly, watching as he opened the door to his small ranch house. Very quickly, she scooted inside before he had a chance to close it. The interior was sparsely furnished, and what furniture there was, was dark, wooden and massive. It suited him, she thought. She turned to look up at him. "I'm Greer Lawford—"

She got no further than that. Rafe raised one brow quizzically as he looked at her.

"Greer?" It sounded like the name of some long-ago screen siren. "What kind of a name is that?"

"A short one," Greer answered tersely.

She gripped her briefcase more tightly, her knuckles aching a little. The man looked like one of those rough-and-tumble cowboys who used to populate the Saturday morning serial westerns of long ago. The kind who brooked no nonsense and listened only to his inner voice, rather than to anything anyone around him had to say. An alpha male, carved out of rock. That, no doubt, included his head.

But Mrs. Maitland wanted this man at the party and Greer was bound and determined to prove herself invaluable to the matriarch she had come very quickly to hold in the highest regard.

A look of disinterest and dismissal slipped over his face and he began to walk away from her. Surprised, Greer strode quickly to catch up and placed herself in front of him.

"My name," she continued, "isn't important—"

The look in his green eyes darkened. "And, no offense, unless you're here to hand me a million dollar check, neither is your reason for being here."

He wanted her gone and his temporary solitude restored. Pulling the tails of his work shirt out of his jeans, Rafe started unbuttoning it, figuring that would be the end of it.

Greer blinked at being so summarily dismissed. She tried not to watch the progress his fingers were making with the buttons on his shirt, or take any note of the hard, smooth chest that was beginning to emerge from beneath the parting material.

Feeling just the slightest bit shaky, she cleared her throat. It was obvious the man hadn't gotten the invitation, otherwise he would have guessed the reason for her sudden appearance.

"Aren't you even mildly interested why I'm here?"

"Nope." And he meant it. Being curious just got you in trouble and he'd had more than his share of trouble in his life. Like now. "What I'm interested in is getting cleaned up."

Finished unbuttoning his shirt, Rafe looked at her expectantly. Why wasn't the woman with the improbable name taking her cue and leaving? He couldn't be any clearer about his disinterest unless he gave her the bum's rush.

The woman, her eyes rather wide behind her oversize light-gray-rimmed glasses, remained where she was.

Rafe unnotched his belt and loosened it.

Greer noticed a shift in the temperature within the room. It was definitely getting warmer. She could feel a blush beginning to climb up her body. The embarrassment that caused just heightened the color altering her skin tone.

"Are you planning on getting undressed?" She congratulated herself on not swallowing nervously before she asked the question.

His eyes met hers as he sat down on the arm of the overstuffed wine-colored leather sofa. The aged furniture creaked slightly. Rafe gripped one boot and pulled it off. "Never took a shower with my clothes on if I could help it."

The second boot came off. Her nerve endings frayed a little more as it hit the floor with a thud.

Oh, God, the next minute he was going to take off his jeans. She wasn't sure which way to avert her eyes and called herself an idiot for feeling this unsettled at her age. But the feeling wouldn't leave.

"Please," Greer said rather loudly, her hand on his arm, stilling any further progress that would fuel her embarrassment, "if you'd just hear me out."

He had to admit that he found the pink blush that was even now furiously climbing up her neck rather intriguing as well as amusing. If he'd been given to placing bets, the way his late father had with a remarkable and unalterable passion, Rafe wouldn't have guessed that the pushy woman before him was a blusher. The women of his acquaintance didn't turn pink unless they'd spent too much time in the sun.

Time was running out. Alyssa would be here shortly with Bethany and he wanted to get cleaned up before then. He damn well wouldn't get a chance once he was alone with the toddler. At a little more than one, Bethany had conquered walking a month ago and was into everything from the moment she set foot in the house unless he deposited her in her playpen. He knew he was living on borrowed time. Any day now, Bethany was going to discover a way to escape the small, confining area.

"All right—" he glanced at his watch "—you've got five minutes. Talk."

Despite her background in the high-tech professional world she used to inhabit, Greer wasn't accustomed to talking fast. That was why she enjoyed working for Megan; she liked having time to lay things out.

"You're going to time me?"

"Yup." His eyes returned to his watch. "And you're wasting it."

Like a marathon swimmer who'd heard the gun go off, Greer took a deep breath and plunged in. "I represent Megan Maitland—"

A muscle twisted in Rafe's rigid jaw. "Never heard of her."

The abrupt dismissal pulled her up short. It took Greer a little more than a beat to recover. "She's your aunt."

Rafe moved his shoulders in an indifferent shrug, his eyes flat. As were his feelings regarding that distant side of the family. Contrary to what he'd just said, he had heard of Megan Maitland. And her family. And her clinic. He'd made the connection after tossing away the invitation he'd received in the mail nearly a month ago. He didn't want to get dragged into anything, especially not now.

Denial seemed the best way to go.

"Sorry."

Greer supposed it was possible that the man hadn't heard of Megan Maitland. If he'd been living in a cave for the last twenty-five years. Still, it wasn't her place to call him a liar.

Ever the diplomat, she pretended she believed him and patiently explained, "She and her family run Maitland Maternity in Austin, Texas."

Greer watched his generous lips draw together in slight disdain. She couldn't tell if it was in response to her, her tone, or what she'd just said.

"I know where Austin is. Don't know where the Maternity is and don't rightly think I'll be needing that information anytime soon." He peeled off his thick gray socks and let them drop over his discarded boots.

Panic made a second appearance, assaulting her stomach. Any second, the man was going to start taking off his jeans, she just knew it. Desperation fueled her determination. "Will you listen to me and stop talking for a minute?"

Rafe's eyes gave nothing away as he offered her a small salute. "Yes, ma'am."

Greer pressed her lips together, trying not to dwell on how much she despised hearing that term applied to her. She'd heard it, time and again, years before she ever thought she deserved it. Years before she was ready for it. She hated the idea that she'd grown into a "ma'am" without ever having been a "miss" in anyone's eyes. She couldn't help feeling that somehow she'd arrived on the doorstep of settled maturity without having reaped the joys of youth along the way.

"Mrs. Maitland is throwing a Christmas party this December—"

Rafe snorted disparagingly. That was no concern of his. "Good time for it."

Greer purposely ignored the blatant disdain in his voice. "—and she'd like you to attend. Actually, she'd like you to arrive there as early as possible so that she could get to know you."

Standing up, he towered over her. His eyes holding hers, Rafe shoved his hands into his pockets. It caused his unsnapped jeans to sink dangerously low on hips that seemed rock solid.

"Why me?"

Her mouth went dry. Greer was having a great deal of difficulty in not noticing just how lean and hard Rafe Maitland was, how his years in the saddle had left him with a body that seemed sculpted out of granite.

Greer dropped her eyes to study the lone pillow

haphazardly thrown onto the sofa, pretending to be interested in its Navajo pattern.

"Well, not you alone. You and all the other Maitlands." She raised her head and looked up at him, wondering if his older brother and sister were going to be this difficult. "Mrs. Maitland wants this to be a family reunion."

He'd just bet she did. Rafe scowled. Well, he had better things to do than dance like a wooden puppet because some rich dowager wanted to amuse herself and pull the strings.

"Sorry, I'm not much on family and I've got all I can handle at the moment." His fingers resting on the tongue of his zipper, Rafe looked at Megan Maitland's messenger, feeling the last of his patience leaving. "Now, if that's all…"

Greer knew that part of her problem was that she appeared to be a complete pushover. But, in a way, that was also part of her strength, her secret weapon, because no one expected her to doggedly dig in. And she did. "No, that's not all. You're supposed to say yes."

Now she was getting him angry. "Why? Because some rich lady says I am?"

Greer's chin rose triumphantly. "Then you do know who she is."

For a second, his attention fixed on the hint of a cleft in Greer's chin. He shook off the sudden, un-

expected impulse to run his finger along the inden-
tation. He'd made a slip and he didn't like making
slips. Making slips was sloppy.

His brows drew together as his eyes darkened.
Lesser men had backed down from him when he
looked like that. That she didn't look afraid both
surprised and impressed him. But impressed or not,
he didn't have time for any nonsense, and this very
definitely came under the heading of "nonsense."

"Whether I do or don't doesn't make any difference. I don't have time for parties, or for sitting
around twiddling my thumbs because some woman
claiming to be my aunt wants to 'get to know me.'"
He shot her words back at her. Rafe had no use for
people who didn't do an honest day's work for a
living. That had been his father's way, living off
others. Scamming, conniving, until the day he met
his demise in an alley behind a casino in what had
all the earmarks of a syndicate hit. "In case you
hadn't noticed, this is a working ranch and I'm one
of the ones doing the working."

Standing over her, he was so close that he
seemed to be taking up all the available air. Determined to make him agree, Greer was still having
trouble keeping her mind focused.

"Mr. Maitland, Mrs. Maitland has her heart set
on getting everyone together."

What some society woman did or didn't want

made no impression on him. He had to make his living out here, in the real world. He turned away from Megan Maitland's little pit bull of a messenger and began to walk toward his bedroom and the shower that was just beyond.

"Well, then, I'm afraid her heart's going to be broken, but I suspect she'll live."

Moving quickly, Greer got in front of him again, blocking his way out of the room. "Why don't you at least think about it?"

Rafe paused, cocked his head as if shifting something over from one side to the other, then said, "There. I thought about it." He looked her right in the eyes. "No," he enunciated very firmly.

She felt her knees becoming less than solid. Envisioning Megan's disappointment, Greer somehow managed to hold her ground. "Why?"

What was wrong with this woman? Why couldn't she take no for an answer? "Because I plain don't have the time or the inclination." He had to really work to hold on to his temper. "Look, I don't know this woman, and if she's my aunt like you say—"

"She is—"

The look in his eyes froze any further words in her throat. "Then where was she before?"

"Before?" Greer echoed, not sure what he was referring to.

"Before now," he ground out. He was tired, he

was hungry and the unseasonable humidity was making the shoulder he'd injured years ago when he'd spilled off his horse ache. "Why no cards at Christmas? Why no visits in the last twenty-five years? No word while I was growing up? For all I know, *Greer,* this is just some big hoax—"

The flash of temper came out of nowhere, like a quick summer storm in the desert. She didn't like the way he'd said her name, as if it were something comical. "It's not."

"Why should I go?" he wanted to know, looming over her again, his eyes holding hers. "Because you say so?"

She was utterly aware of him. The youngest of Mrs. Maitland's long lost family was standing much too close to her. The fact that he was also bare-chested and sweaty was making it increasingly difficult for her to breathe. Telling herself that it was the heavy September air and not the man was a flat-out lie and she knew it.

Still, like a loyal terrier, she hung in. "No, because it's the right thing to do."

The right thing. What did someone with smooth, pampered hands and unbroken fingernails know about the right thing? What would she know about how hard it was to make a living in a hostile world? His lips curled in a sneer.

"The right thing, *Greer,* would be for you to

retreat and tell Her Majesty that one of her relatives can't be summoned to the gathering." He paused at his bedroom door, his hand on the doorknob. "I'm sure I won't be the only one sending his 'regrets.'"

She wasn't accustomed to lying, but she was beginning to think that perhaps there was a time and a place for everything.

"Yes, you will be," Greer called after him.

He laughed under his breath and then turned to look at her over his shoulder, sincerely doubting her statement. "Well, I always did like standing out. Now, you've used up your five minutes, Greer, and I'd like to get on a first-name basis with my shower, so I figure you can see yourself out."

With that he withdrew, leaving her flabbergasted and alone in his living room.

He shed his jeans as he walked toward his bathroom shower stall. Damn, where did she get off, being pushy like that? He had a hell of a lot more important things on his mind than prancing off to some society bigwig's party and being treated like the long lost black sheep of the family.

Rafe turned on the water full blast and let the steam envelop him, kneading the tight, aching muscles.

Tilting his head up under the showerhead, he laughed to himself. Hell, the whole side of his family could be thought of as black sheep when it came to the Maitland clan. And he supposed he was the blackest for not having anything to do with any of them.

But there were reasons for that.

Besides, he thought, lathering quickly, he had more than enough to deal with, what with Rory and Lil dying and leaving him to care for Bethany. Him, a confirmed bachelor without a clue what to do with a baby that didn't have four legs and a tail. If that wasn't enough, Lil's aunt and uncle had suddenly turned up after years of silence, demanding custody of the little girl.

He washed the soap from his body, turning up the heat another notch and standing there to absorb the hot water. Maybe he would even have let them have Bethany, if he hadn't given his word to Lil that he wouldn't. With almost the last breath in her body, she'd begged him not to let the pair get their hands on Bethany. Not to put her baby through the hell she'd lived through and barely survived as a child. Lil wanted something better for Bethany. And it was up to him to see that she got it.

So he'd gone to a lawyer, first thing, and plunked down his hard-earned money, knowing that he needed help to allow him to keep his word. That stuck in his throat a little, not being able to do it alone. He was used to fighting his own battles, cleaning up his own messes. He'd been doing it ever since he could remember, raising himself because his parents were either too busy fighting or too busy living their own lives to take any notice of him.

Well, strictly speaking, he supposed his mother had tried her best. But the former showgirl was far more suited to dancing in skimpy outfits than to being a mother. She hadn't the faintest idea what a kid needed. But Veronica Maitland had given him love and he supposed she had done her best.

He didn't fault her. He faulted his father, who actually *was* a Maitland. In Rafe's book, they were all probably like his old man. Out for themselves, self-serving. There had to be some kind of gimmick behind this invitation, he thought, and he wasn't about to play along. Not if there wasn't anything in it for him.

As seductive as standing under the shower was, Rafe forced himself to hurry. He didn't want to greet the new cook's daughter in his birthday suit. He'd seen the way the cook could swing a cleaver and wanted to take no chances on being on the receiving end of that.

Getting out, Rafe quickly toweled himself dry and slid on a clean pair of jeans. Alyssa, he figured, would be here with the baby any minute. They had an arrangement. She watched the baby during the day while he worked, and he was teaching her to ride. He figured he was getting the better end of the deal.

His hair still damp from the shower, his clean shirt only half buttoned, Rafe opened his bedroom door and walked out of the room to find that the woman in the large glasses and sensible shoes was once again standing in his living room.

"What the hell are you doing back?" he demanded.

Her back to him, Greer jumped, startled. She hadn't heard the door open. She'd been waiting for him, trying to string together her words so that she could make an effective argument, and he'd surprised her.

She bit her lower lip. She was better at delivering an argument on paper than in person, but it was time she learned how to talk.

"I never left."

Rafe indicated the door behind her. "Well, leave now."

She stood her ground. "No, not until you actually hear me out." *And not until you say yes,* she added silently. She began to talk quickly, knowing he was getting ready to cut her off. "The reason Mrs. Maitland never got in contact with you before is that, until just recently, she was as ignorant of you as you were of her. The point is—" Greer drew herself up "—you know about each other now and now is all that counts."

He'd always admired guts, and he had to admit, she seemed to have guts in spades. Instead of throwing the woman out, he rethought the situation. If he gave her a condition she couldn't meet, she'd be forced to withdraw and stop badgering him. And his conscience would be clean.

"You're right," he agreed. "Now is all that counts. If you're so hot to get me there, fine. But I need a favor." He leveled his gaze at her. *"Now."*

The nervousness she'd been experiencing ever since she'd seen him walking toward her like a stalking panther intensified.

"What kind of favor?" She failed to keep the tension out of her voice.

A fragment of what the lawyer he'd gone to had said to him came back to Rafe. The attorney had told him that he would have an easier time of gaining custody of Bethany if he was married or at least engaged.

Okay, that was it. He looked at her. "I need a fiancée."

It was to Greer's credit that her mouth didn't drop open. "I beg your pardon?"

He had her, Rafe thought triumphantly. He could almost hear the door closing behind her already.

"No need to beg anything. I made a promise to

two friends, the best friends a man could ever want, and in order to keep that promise, it looks like I'm going to need a fiancée. A wife, really, but I don't think I have to carry this act too far.'' She was going to turn tail and run any second, he promised himself. ''Tell me, Greer, do you want me to go to this Christmas thing enough to pretend to be my fiancée?''

This was insane. What he was asking was plain crazy. It went way above and beyond the call of duty to the point of being absurd. A fiancée.

She had no idea why she was even considering it.

Because, a tiny voice within her whispered, in all likelihood, this was going to be the closest she would ever get to being anyone's fiancée or to wearing an engagement ring, other than staring at one through Tiffany's window.

Besides, more than likely, the man was bluffing. If she met his bluff, he'd be forced to give in and give up. She smiled at him with a shade of triumph. She had him.

''Yes.''

She saw surprise register on his lean, tanned face, followed by shock. Greer congratulated herself on guessing correctly.

Self-congratulations were short-lived as she saw a smile beginning at the corners of his mouth.

Though it was a small smile, it seemed to make all the difference in the world. His austere face turned heart-stoppingly handsome.

Greer felt her heart go into double-time before she could think to rein it in. The air turned several degrees warmer than it already was.

An uneasiness began to spread through her. What in heaven's name had she just gotten herself into?

Chapter 2

Okay, Rafe thought, his mind racing as he pieced things together, realigning them in light of what had just transpired, maybe this whole reunion idea might actually work out to his benefit. His, and more important, Bethany's.

Until the lady with the ridiculous name had pushed him a little too hard, he hadn't been thinking along the lines of deception, but hell, he'd learned a long time ago that when an avalanche of lemons starts tumbling your way, you had damn well better learn how to make lemonade out of them fast.

This, he decided, was going to be lemonade.

All right, this was going to be a lie, he allowed, but it wasn't the kind of lie his father habitually told. This was going to be a lie for a good purpose, and sometimes the end did justify the means. Especially if that end meant that he got to keep Bethany.

What he needed right now was a little something extra in his corner to tip the scales. After all, this was Lil's uncle and aunt he was taking on in the courtroom, not her parents or grandparents, both of whom, had they been alive, would have had a lot more leverage than he did in the eyes of the court. The odds became a tiny bit better when the family connection was a little more distant, as it was in this case. If he had a few chips stacked on his side, he might just win this fight. And he needed to win, because he'd given his word.

And because Bethany had already won his heart. He couldn't rightly see life without her anymore.

The first thing he had to do, he knew even without the attorney's advice, was to make himself seem respectable and stable in the eyes of the family court judge. Never mind that he'd turned his life around these last few years, going from being a rootless hellion to a man who made a decent living as a foreman on a large ranch. He'd worked his way up to that, spending long, hard hours doing anything that needed doing and learning the ranching business while he was at it. Eventually, he intended to own his own horse ranch, but for now, he was content to work his butt off for a boss who was demanding but fair.

There was no doubt about it, he was nothing like the no-account gambler from Las Vegas he'd been on his way to becoming—just like his father.

But none of that really mattered. According to the lawyer he'd recently hired, what seemed to count heavily in the eyes of the court was his marital status. That and his standing in the community. He didn't have much of a reputation in the community, keeping to himself whenever possible, and there was no way to turn himself into a pillar of that community in a short amount of time.

But he could pretend to be on his way to getting married. And, he'd only just realized, he did have connections that counted. Connections this slim-hipped, no-frills woman standing in his living room had just made him acutely aware of. Connections that just might help turn the tide for him.

Rafe widened his smile.

As a rule, he didn't believe in riding on anyone else's coattails. He'd gotten to where he was by relying only on himself ever since he'd been half his age. But rules wouldn't be rules if they weren't sometimes bent a little.

Even so, he wouldn't be considering this under

ordinary circumstances. But these weren't ordinary circumstances. He had Bethany's welfare to consider.

The pint-size little darling had been the center of Rory and Lil's world and had quickly taken over that spot in his. If even half the things that Lil had said about her childhood were true, there was no way on God's green earth he was going to allow Bethany to fall into the hands of Lil's uncle and aunt. Lil had grown up in a world devoid of love and caring. He wanted Bethany to have a happy childhood, not an emotionally deprived one.

If achieving that goal meant having to be friendly with a woman who hadn't given him, or his family for that matter, the time of day in all these years, he was up to it. He could play the game and pretend, ultimately giving Megan Maitland exactly what she deserved. Nothing. All things considered, the charade seemed like a small price to pay for Bethany's welfare.

Rafe shoved his hands into his back pockets, straining the jeans against his hips. Very slowly, he circled Greer, studying her intently. She looked a little skittish to him. He'd seen horses with that look, all spit and polish on the outside but ready to bolt at the first loud sound they heard.

The last thing he wanted was to have her fold on him when the going got tough.

Rafe drew closer to Greer, still scrutinizing her. He watched her face. "You're sure about this?"

She knew it. He was waiting for her to back down. Confidence began to return. This wasn't really any different than a merger or an acquisition.

Except that mergers and acquisitions never wore worn, tight-fitting jeans that caused her mind to lose its focus and her pulse to do funny things.

Blocking out the sight, Greer raised her chin defiantly.

"I'm sure."

"Great, you've got yourself a houseguest."

Rafe put his hand out to hers. When she didn't take it quickly enough, he took hers and wrapped his tanned fingers around it, gripping firmly. To his surprise, the limp handshake he expected didn't materialize. Instead, after a beat, his mysterious aunt's emissary shook his hand as firmly as any man he'd ever made a bargain with.

A handshake said a lot about a person. Maybe there was hope for the woman yet.

Those same nerves she'd felt earlier began to waltz through her again, picking up the tempo until they could have been accused of doing an old-fashioned jitterbug instead. They were especially prevalent along her arm. The arm that was connected to the hand that had been swallowed up by his.

It was all she could do to return the pressure of his grip. She knew he'd respect nothing less.

Taking care not to pull her hand away from his too quickly and give Rafe the impression that she was leery of him, Greer extricated her hand as she tried to sort out any misunderstandings before they had a chance to mushroom out of control.

"You're not going to be my houseguest, you'll be staying with Mrs. Maitland. The estate has a great many guest rooms."

The smile on his lips moved slowly until it lit his face. Rafe knew exactly what she was thinking, though she was doing an admirable job of attempting to mask it. He'd come across fear more than once or twice himself and he was able to recognize the signs.

"This engagement is just for appearances. You don't have anything to worry about."

She'd be the judge of that. Men who looked like Rafe Maitland were always dangerous.

"Do you mind if I ask why you need a fiancée?" She raised her hands before he had a chance to accuse her of backing down. "Not that I'm reneging, I just need a few details if I'm going to be convincing in this part."

Rafe caught himself watching her mouth as she spoke and looked up into her eyes instead. Her choice of words amused him. *Convincing.* Now, that was something that could lead to a great many interesting things. If he were in the market for that kind of thing. A couple of years ago, he might have been. But his wild days and his wild oats were all behind him. They had to be. He had a good job, a future and a baby to worry about. Women were the last thing to occupy his thoughts.

But before he could answer her, there was a knock on his front door. The next minute, it was being opened.

The dark-haired woman with the snapping brown eyes and the easy smile who entered was obviously not worried about standing on ceremony, Greer thought as she turned to see her walk in. She had a baby with her comfortably resting on her hip. The baby had dark hair, like she did.

The familiar way the woman looked at Rafe made Greer think they had an intimate relationship. Was she his girlfriend? His mistress? And why was he asking her to pose as his fiancée when this spit-fire was part of his life?

Greer squared her shoulders, feeling suddenly dowdy and lifeless despite the designer suit she had so carefully selected for her trip out here.

The woman flashed a smile at him, then at her. "Sorry, Rafe, I didn't realize you had company."

To Greer's surprise, she saw him reaching for the woman's baby. Was the little girl his? Why hadn't

Mrs. Maitland mentioned that he had a child? It didn't seem like the type of oversight she'd make, given how she felt about children.

Maybe Mrs. Maitland hadn't known, she realized.

Greer had the feeling that she was slipping deeper down the rabbit hole. What she needed right now was a rabbit with answers.

He could almost see the questions in Greer's eyes. She was chewing on her lower lip, as if to bite them back.

"This isn't company," he told the woman as he took Bethany into his arms. "This is Greer." He figured it was enough of an explanation. Rafe brushed a kiss against the top of the baby's head. "So, how're you doing, honey? Did you have a good day?"

In response, the baby made a cooing noise and he smiled as if she'd answered him. He tucked her against him comfortably. The little girl contented herself with playing with the buttons on his shirt.

Taking the initiative, the woman stepped forward and took Greer's hand in hers. Her smile was genuine even as she swept her eyes over Greer, making a quick appraisal.

"Hello, I'm Alyssa Martinez." She inclined her head to indicate somewhere beyond the small ranch house. "I help my father with the cooking at the main house, when I'm not watching Bethany. She's a regular pistol, this one.''

Greer returned the handshake before dropping her hand to her side. For a second, she couldn't think of anything to say. Women like Alyssa Martinez had been making her feel inferior all of her life. Not deliberately, they did it just by existing. They were bold, vital, and everything looked good on them. So did nothing. Alyssa's obvious curves, even beneath the peasant blouse and wide skirt she wore, made Greer acutely aware of her almost boyish figure.

Oh, sure, she worked out when she could find the time and that kept her body lean and toned, but it never coaxed forward any curves. For that miracle to occur, she would have had to have submitted to a surgeon's scalpel and she wasn't about to do that.

Besides, there was no one to do it for, so the point, even if she had been inclined to consider it, was a moot one. There was no one to make herself pretty for, no one to keep in mind when she shopped for clothes. The items in her closet were all tasteful and from the best stores, but they lacked imagination and color. She didn't see the need for it.

"Can't make a silk purse out of a sow's ear," Mrs. Malone had told her more than once while she was growing up. Mrs. Malone had run the children's shelter where she had spent most of her youth, and the message had stuck that much more because Mrs. Malone had meant it to be kind. To prevent her from being set up for any future disappointments. "A girl has to know her limits, you know," she'd firmly asserted.

And Greer knew hers.

"I'm Greer Lawford," Greer finally said, retreating to the persona she was most comfortable with, the one she had created when she'd forged out into the corporate world. That Greer was strong and confident, good at whatever she did no matter what it was she chose to do.

In high school she'd discovered that she had an aptitude for learning, and ever since, she had made a point of acquainting herself with whatever world she ventured into. Not just learning about it but mastering it. Like a person deprived of one sense, she made the others that much more sensitive and acute in order to compensate. In her case, she figured that what she lacked was looks. She was determined to make up for it with brains.

And by making herself indispensable to the person she worked for. Which was why she was here when she would much rather be behind a desk, manning phones and pulling together the two hundred and twenty-nine different strings that were involved in making this holiday reunion a success.

She forced herself to return Alyssa's smile. "I work for Mrs. Megan Maitland."

Alyssa looked at Rafe. "Maitland. Is that your mother?"

Bethany was trying to chew on one of his buttons. Rafe drew it away from her mouth. "My aunt, according to Greer."

Why was it that every time he said her name, she had the impression he was going to follow it with a full-bellied laugh? Greer wasn't that ridiculous a name, she thought defensively.

Alyssa looked surprised and oddly tickled. "Hey, I didn't know you had a family."

Rafe shrugged dismissively. He didn't really like talking about any of his family.

"A very large family," Greer said before Rafe had the opportunity to say anything. She had a feeling there was a disclaimer on his lips and she didn't want to give him a chance to utter it. "And Mrs. Maitland wants to gather everyone together in Texas for a big family celebration this year."

Her arms devoid of the baby, Alyssa smoothed down her shirt and looked at Rafe with what appeared to be a touch of hope. "Sounds like fun. You going to go?"

Afraid he was going to say no, Greer jumped in to answer. "Yes, he is."

Dark brows drew together over a nose that could

almost be called delicate. Greer wondered if he re-
sembled his mother or his father.

"Don't get carried away with this engagement
thing," he warned her. "I can still do my own talking and my own answering."

"Engagement?" Alyssa echoed. Curiosity quickly painted itself across her fine features along with
more than a touch of disappointment. "When did
all this happen?"

"It didn't," Rafe told her, switching Bethany to
his other side. The area around half his buttons was
wet from the toddler's questing mouth and grasping
fingers. "I figured an 'engagement' was the best
way to keep Bethany and my word to Rory and
Lil."

"But it's not real." Alyssa sounded as if she
wanted to make perfectly certain of that fact.

"No, it's not real," Rafe assured her.

"Oh." Alyssa nodded, obviously understanding
what he was saying.

But she didn't, Greer thought, and she decided it
was time someone filled her in. She turned, looking
at Rafe. "I think we've come full circle, Mr. Maitland."

"I think if we're going to be engaged, you'd better call me Rafe. And," he added, shaking his head
at Bethany, who was once again reaching for his
shirt and the fascinating buttons, "you'd better

learn how to talk a whole lot plainer than that.''
Rafe looked at Greer, his brow raised. "What do
you mean, full circle?"

She could feel Alyssa studying her. Her discomfort grew. "Well, I asked you to explain to me why
you need a fiancée and you were about to tell me
when the door opened." She spared Alyssa a
glance.

To underscore his point, Rafe grasped Bethany
by the waist with both hands and held her up. The
little girl laughed and cooed, then clapped her hands
as if this were a familiar game between them.

"This—" he nodded at Bethany "—is why I
need a fiancée."

Greer still wasn't quite following him. "Your
daughter?"

"Not yet." Lowering her, he tucked Bethany
against him again with a practiced movement Greer
found intriguing. Most men she knew were uncomfortable with children that size. "But she will be
once I can file adoption papers." His face grew
grave. "In order to do that, I have to have clear
claim to her."

"And you don't," Greer guessed. For someone
who gave the impression that he was a man of few
words, he certainly seemed to like stretching things
out.

He scowled, thinking of the threat that Lil's relatives posed. "No, not right now."

Still confused, Greer looked to the other woman for a further explanation, but there was no enlightenment coming from that quarter.

"I'd better be getting back," Alyssa announced suddenly, as if she'd just become aware of the time. "I have to be putting dinner on the table soon. Mr. Owen doesn't like to be kept waiting. If you need *anything*—" she underlined the word, looking at Rafe "—just call. Nice meeting you," she added as an afterthought, glancing at Greer. The next moment, Alyssa slipped out the front door.

"Same here," Greer murmured, her voice utterly flat.

Rafe caught the uncomfortable note in her voice and looked at her curiously.

She didn't care for the way he seemed to be continually scrutinizing her. It made her feel awkward, as if she were found wanting. To get his attention off her and back to her yet unanswered questions, Greer nodded at Bethany. "Whose baby is that?"

Because of the hour, Bethany had begun settling down. He knew that Alyssa had already changed and fed her. He stroked the fine, dark hair. "She belonged to Lil and Rory Butler."

Greer picked up on the past tense. "The friends you mentioned earlier?"

"You were paying attention." A minor smile gracing his lips, Rafe nodded his approval.

If there was one thing these schoolmarm types were, it was sticklers for detail. He figured that having her in the courtroom as his fiancée might impress the judge enough to make him see things Rafe's way. After all, he was young, with his whole life in front of him, and the Prestons were well past their primes. Too old to be taking care of a one-year-old, really, he reasoned.

"I *always* pay attention," she informed him.

He didn't like the coolness in her voice. You would have thought he'd insulted her.

"Good." His voice was crisp, matching hers. "Then I won't have to repeat myself. Lil and Rory were killed in a car accident a little more than a month ago. I always knew they wanted me to be Bethany's guardian, but it's not really the kind of thing you pay attention to when the people you're talking to are twenty-three years old and in perfect health."

If he had paid attention, maybe he would have tried to talk them out of it, he thought. Tried to make them pick someone else who could give Bethany more than he could. But what was done was done and, Rafe had to admit, he doubted if anyone could care as much for the little girl as he did.

"Anyway, after the accident I took Bethany in,

and not long after that, I heard from some guy claiming that he represented Lil's aunt and uncle and that they were coming for the baby.''

Most men she knew would have been relieved to relinquish the responsibility of raising a toddler. Especially alone. Her own mother had seen fit to leave her sitting alone in the last pew of a church when she was barely three. That was where she was told they'd found her. Curled up, asleep in a pew with only the clothes on her back and a battered stuffed animal that was so worn it was unidentifiable.

''That would make things easier for you.''

He couldn't quite read her comment. She wasn't one of these liberated females who looked down their noses at families, was she? Not that it mattered if she played her part right.

If.

That was the all-important word.

Of course, if he could find the softer side of Megan Maitland, he might be able to get the woman to use her influence and settle things for him, then there'd be no need to continue the engagement charade.

The thought of using his aunt's influence didn't sit well with him, even though he wasn't planning to use it for any personal monetary gain.

Because it raised issues he just didn't have time

to sort through, Rafe put the whole thing out of his mind for now.

"Sometimes 'easy' isn't the best way. I gave my word and I intend to stick by it."

Rafe didn't add that giving Bethany up would create a giant-size hole in his heart. The little girl had created a space for herself that he'd never expected to be there. He wasn't given to attachments or bonding. But he had bonded with the little lady in his arms and he intended to do right by her. No matter what it took or what it cost him.

This wasn't making any sense to Greer. "And you honestly think that by lying to the court, you'll get to retain custody?"

He didn't like being judged. Especially not by a stranger who had no idea what was involved. His eyes grew flinty as he looked at her. "Call it a stopgap maneuver. Until I can come up with something better."

Her breath caught in her throat. There was no reason to feel as though she'd just been put in her place, and yet she did.

"It's not a bad idea," Greer said, backpedaling in case Mrs. Maitland's long lost nephew thought she was criticizing him. She didn't want to take a chance on losing him after she'd gotten him to agree to come, albeit with an unusual addendum. "But why didn't you ask Alyssa to pretend to be your fiancée?'' In Greer's estimation, the fiery-looking woman would have been far more believable in the role. Rafe and Alyssa looked as if they belonged together.

Quite simply, the answer was that he'd only just now thought of the ruse. And asking Alyssa to pose as his fiancée might get sticky. He knew she had more than a passing liking for him, and while he was flattered, he didn't want to get his life tangled up with anyone else's at present. Bethany was the only female he could safely handle for the time being.

Rafe took the easy way out. ''Because she's not asking me to go off to Austin and pretend to be happy about some reunion.''

They seemed doomed to continue getting off on the wrong foot. ''I'm not asking you to pretend to be happy about it—''

''Good, one less thing to do.'' Bethany began fussing against him. He'd gotten good at telling the different noises apart. This one meant she was sleepy.

''I think you're going about this all wrong.''

Didn't this woman every stop flapping her gums? ''And 'this' would be…?''

''The Christmas reunion.'' She was beginning to think he was deliberately being difficult. ''It's supposed to be fun.''

"I'll put on my happy face," he promised her, sarcasm tingeing his words. And then he thought of something. They couldn't just say they were engaged and expect the judge to believe them. He needed something to serve as outward proof that he was serious.

"Here, hold her for a minute."

Not waiting for Greer to say anything, he thrust the baby toward her.

Surprised, Greer had no choice but to take the fussing baby into arms that were far more adept at holding on to stacks of tightly bound quarterly financial reports.

Then, to her further dismay, Rafe walked away from her.

"Where are you going?" she called after him. The baby squirmed in her arms.

"To get something" was all he said.

As Greer tried to hold on to Bethany without dropping her, her dismay deepened. This time it was a pint-size fiery womanette who was making her feel that she was decidedly out of her element. Large or small, the end result was the same.

With a sigh, Greer looked toward the room that Rafe had disappeared into. Now what?

Chapter 3

Once in his bedroom, it took Rafe only a few seconds to locate what he was looking for. The item was just where he'd left it, tucked in the back of the top drawer of the lone nightstand that stood by his bed. He'd never thought he'd have any use for it.

Taking it out, he rubbed his thumb over the top of the black velvet box. Strange the way some things worked out. When he'd won this from Albert Hackett that long weekend he, Albert and a couple of the other hands had played poker until dawn, he'd had every intention of going into town and selling it at the pawnshop the first chance he got.

At the time, he'd had no more use for an engagement ring than Albert had. But he'd never gotten around to selling it and now, it looked as if that was a good thing. The ring was going to come in handy.

Closing the drawer, he walked back out into the living room and then stopped dead. If he'd ever seen anyone who looked more awkward than this woman as she tried to hold Bethany, he certainly couldn't recall it. He didn't think that even he'd been this ungainly the first time Lil had had him hold the baby. Weren't women supposed to have some kind of a natural instinct when it came to babies? If so, someone must have forgotten to tell the Lawford woman that.

He shook his head as he crossed to Greer. It was a wonder she hadn't dropped Bethany.

"You're holding her like she was a sack of solidified sugar." She looked as if his comment embarrassed her. That hadn't been his intention and it chafed his conscience a little, which made him all the more short-tempered. "Haven't you ever held a baby before?"

Greer turned toward him, relieved that he'd returned. Afraid of dropping Bethany, she'd begun to wonder if he was ever coming back. She had no idea that babies wiggled so much. The shrug was careless and self-conscious.

"No. It was never part of my job description."

He held off taking Bethany for a minute, amused at the way Greer was holding the baby out to him, as if she were a wriggling snake that could at any moment turn and bite her. "Only child?" he guessed.

Something within her darkened. She wasn't here to discuss her background, or the lack of it.

"Something like that." Why was he just looking at her? Why wasn't he taking the baby? "Would you like to take your daughter-to-be back?"

"Sure, I'll trade you."

It was then that she saw he was holding a small black velvet box in his hand. The kind rings were found in. But that was silly. It seemed odd that Rafe had an engagement ring just lying around. It wasn't as if it was a spare tire or an extra pair of jeans to be kept around in case of emergencies. The kind of rings that were housed in velvet boxes were expensive.

"All right." Gingerly, she began to negotiate the transfer. Just then, Bethany grabbed a strand of her hair and wound her fingers around it tightly. As the baby pulled hard, tears of pain sprang to Greer's eyes. "Ow!"

"Hold it," he warned. "I think we've got a snag here."

Think? "What was your first clue?" Greer all but yelped.

Rafe laughed under his breath in response. Holding Bethany in the crook of his arm, the velvet box in the same hand, he used his free one to extricate Greer's hair from Bethany's grasp. For a baby, Bethany had a pretty strong grip. Like her dad, Rafe thought, sadness spearing him.

He took a step back in case Bethany tried to make another grab for Greer. The hair she'd clutched remained all stuck together.

He grinned. "I think you might want to wash that. Looks like Alyssa gave her something sticky to play with just before she brought her over."

"Terrific," Greer muttered.

Gingerly, she ran her fingers over the strand of hair that had been rescued. Rafe was right. It was decidedly sticky. Candy sticky. She probably looked like something straight out of a Halloween night, Greer thought glumly. Battling mushrooming embarrassment, Greer tried to smooth down the stiff strand of hair with her hand and knew she was probably only making things worse. She couldn't wait to get back to her hotel room and take a hot shower. An extra-long hot shower to work all this tension out of her shoulders. Not to mention the rest of her.

"Maybe you'd like to wash your hands," he sug-

gested. Not waiting for an answer, Rafe led the way
to his bedroom. Opening the door, he kicked aside
the pair of jeans he'd left on the floor. "Bathroom's
right through there." He pointed toward the open
door at the far end of the room.

"Thanks."

Walking into the room, she was exceedingly conscious of being in a man's bedroom. It wasn't
something she was even remotely familiar with.
The only men she had come in contact with until
recently all wore three-piece suits and faced her
across a boardroom table, not a bedroom.

She tried not to pay attention to the rumpled,
unmade bed with its comforter dripping down onto
the floor, or the thought of Rafe being in it. She
tried even harder to ignore the jeans he'd kicked
aside, the ones he'd stripped off earlier and left on
the floor on his way to the shower.

Despite her efforts, the maleness of the room insisted on assaulting her from all sides.

Washing her hands quickly, Greer hurried away
from the intimate surroundings as soon as she
could, before their impression could have a chance
to sink in any further than it already had.

When she returned to the living room, she found
Rafe sitting on the sofa. Oblivious to her, he was
busy playing with the baby.

She couldn't help noting how at ease he seemed.

His legs crossed, he was holding Bethany on one knee and jostling her in a simulated pony ride that had the little girl shrieking with delight.

He seemed like the perfect father, she thought. Just showed how initial impressions were deceiving. Seeing him earlier, she would have said that the only place the man could have been at ease was in a saddle.

Or a woman's bed.

The thought snuck up on her, making her cheeks warm before she had a chance to shake it off. Terrific, she thought disdainfully, they were probably pink again. He was going to think she was some kind of trembling, backward vestal virgin.

He glanced up and realized that Greer had walked back into the room and was watching him. Ending the impromptu pony ride, he rose to his feet. With Bethany in his arms, he walked over to a playpen in the corner. Tucked into an alcove that doubled as a makeshift study, complete with a small, second-hand desk, it was almost out of sight.

Looking at it, Greer thought the playpen seemed completely out of place within the very masculine room.

"You stay here for a few minutes, honey," he told the baby. Turning his attention back to Greer, Rafe held out the velvet box he'd gotten from his room. "Here, if you're going to pretend to be my fiancée, I think you might need this."

Greer had no idea why she felt so nervous taking the box from him. After all, this was just pretend. She opened it, and even though it was a typical ring box, she was still surprised when she found herself looking down at the contents.

"It's a ring."

For just a moment, she'd looked like a little girl, afraid of being disappointed at Christmas as she opened the one gift that mattered, he thought.

"Sure it's a ring." He drew a little closer to her, intrigued by her expression. "What did you think it was going to be, a washer?"

"No, but—" Astonished, she raised her eyes to his face. "It's an engagement ring."

She left the rest unspoken, but it was clear that she was having trouble understanding why a cowboy would just happen to have an engagement ring sitting around in his bedroom.

He wasn't sure if he should be taking offense or not. "Yes, so?"

Exasperation flittered through her. Why did he insist on dragging things out? He knew what she was asking him. "So what's a cowboy on a horse ranch in the middle of Nevada doing with an engagement ring in his bedroom bureau?"

"It was in the nightstand," he corrected her. He

saw impatience crease her brow and got a kick out of it. "And civilization has managed to reach here."

She blew out a breath. She wasn't trying to insult him; she was just trying to make sense out of this.

"That's not what I meant. Most people don't just 'happen' to have engagement rings lying around." And then the answer hit her. She'd put her foot into it, hadn't she? It wouldn't be the first time. When it came to her private life, social skills were not exactly high on her list of accomplishments. "Did you...I mean did someone...?"

Damn it, he'd been engaged, she realized, and something had gone wrong and now she was making things worse by artlessly prodding. Why couldn't she just leave well enough alone? She flushed. Her tongue always seemed to fail her when it came to private matters.

He'd never seen that shade of red on a woman's face before.

"No, no one jilted me, if that's what you're getting at. I won the ring in a poker game." He saw her embarrassment ebb away, replaced by a touch of suspicion. He could guess what she was thinking. "Don't worry, it's real. The guy I won it from was the jilted one. Actually, his woman ran off with someone else before he ever had a chance to give it to her properly. He figured hanging on to the ring brought him bad luck.'' That had been Albert's story, but it had come after the man had had more than his share to drink. Rafe laughed shortly under his breath. ''At least it did that night when he was playing poker.''

Greer stared at the orphaned engagement ring for a long moment, words failing her. It was beautiful. Small, it twinkled like a perfect star that had fallen out of the sky.

''Well, don't just keep staring at it, try it on.'' Before she could, Rafe plucked the ring out of its velvet seat. Taking her left hand in his, he slid the ring on her finger. It went on easily. Rafe smiled. ''How about that, it fits.''

The moment he slipped the ring onto her finger, she could feel something tingling all through her body. Like magic.

Silly thought, she upbraided herself. But the feeling didn't go away.

''Yes,'' she answered quietly, ''it does.''

Their eyes met for a moment, and then he released her hand. He slid his own into his back pockets. ''I guess it's official, then. We're engaged.''

She forced a smile to her lips, her stomach churning. She started feeling an odd queasiness. ''When's the wedding?'' When he looked at her in silence, she added, ''That's a joke.''

''Yeah, but people are going to ask that.'' He

thought for a moment. "How about Valentine's Day? Sounds like a good day to get married."

Valentine's Day. Could he have come up with a more romantic thought? Not in her estimation. She looked at the man in amazement.

"Yes, sure. Perfect day."

The words emerged in muted staccato beats as she looked back down at the gleaming globe of fire-light on her finger. The sunlight that filled the room pushed itself into the stone, shooting out beams of yellow, white and blue as she moved her out-stretched hand.

His mouth curved. To look at her, you would have thought that she'd never...

Maybe she never had, he suddenly thought. Maybe there'd never been anyone special in this woman's life, to make *her* feel special. Looking at Greer, he could believe it. The woman was plain, though he had to admit she had beautiful eyes.

Well, whether or not she'd ever been engaged or married didn't make any difference to him. He just needed her services long enough for the family court hearing—or until he got Megan Maitland to throw her support his way. He had a feeling her name could open up a lot of doors, make things easier. If that sounded a little cold, maybe it was, but he'd learned a long time ago that it was best to leave his conscience and emotions at the door when it came to getting necessary things done. They only got in the way in the long run.

Trying hard to get this strange, unsettled feeling traveling through her under some kind of control, Greer dropped her hand to her side. But she fisted it so that she could run her thumb along the edge of the band just to assure herself that the ring was actually there.

Part of her still felt that this was all just a little surreal. She looked at Rafe, summoning her best corporate demeanor, knowing that it was best to keep to business.

"So if I go through with this, pretend to be your fiancée, you're really going to come back to Austin with me? For Mrs. Maitland's reunion?" she added.

She knew she was repeating herself, but she wanted to make absolutely certain that there was no room for a misunderstanding. Or grounds for him to back down.

With a sensible-looking woman like this at his side, the judge was certain to think he would make a stable home for Bethany, Rafe thought. "How soon would I have to leave?"

Greer hesitated for a moment. She knew Mrs. Maitland's preferences, but she wasn't sure how they would go over with Rafe. "Actually, she was hoping to meet you as soon as possible."

Was the woman crazy? "This is September. Just how long a celebration was she planning?"

But then, he supposed cynically, what else did rich people who didn't have to work for a living have to do with themselves? She probably partied continually.

Greer did her best to ignore the sarcasm in Rafe's voice.

"Mrs. Maitland realizes that you can't just pick up and go somewhere for three months, but she was hoping you might be able to come to Austin for a short visit and then return for the reunion in December. She'd like you to meet the rest of the family."

Having pulled herself up onto her feet, Bethany was rattling the sides of her playpen, signaling that she thought she'd been ignored long enough. Rafe crossed to the little girl and bent over the playpen to pick her up. Only then did he turn to Greer.

"Why?"

He was being antagonistic again. She had thought they'd gotten past this part. Obviously not. Greer reverted to her role of chief assistant, leaving behind her own persona, the one that caused her to appear so ineffectual. It was a great deal easier for her to operate as if she were devoid of feelings.

"Because family has always been extremely important to Mrs. Maitland. She understands what it's like to be alone…''

Rafe looked at her sharply. He had absolutely no patience with people who were given to pretense. ''Yeah, right.''

Greer immediately leaped to the defense of the woman she'd grown to admire so deeply in such a short amount of time. Megan Maitland was everything she'd ever wanted to be: confident, kind, generous and well respected in addition to being well liked.

''No, really.'' She followed Rafe and the baby to the sofa. ''She's lived through a great deal in her life and she didn't always have it easy—''

Rafe raised his eyebrows in mock sympathy. ''What, the dilemma of which party to go to, what dress to wear to what ball?''

The smirk on his face irritated her beyond words. Greer was surprised by her own reaction. She didn't ordinarily become incensed so quickly. ''You always ride around with that chip on your shoulder?''

He began to tell her what she could do with her opinion but caught himself just in time. There was a baby present and he wasn't about to use strong language around her. ''Hey, any chips I have, I came by honestly.''

''So did your aunt, except she doesn't wear them.'' Because he didn't immediately jump in with a retort, she hurried to continue. "At seventeen, she was poorer than dirt and working for a living...."

He was certain that this woman's definition of *poor* differed from his own. Despite her colorful description, he had his doubts about how poor his aunt had been. After all, William Maitland wouldn't have thrown his lot in with some waif or bimbo.

"Well, she certainly has worked her way up into the lap of luxury, hasn't she?"

The irritated look on her face gave way to a knowing one. Rafe had lied to her when he'd claimed that he didn't know who Megan Maitland or any of the Maitlands were. He'd just proved it.

"Then you really do know who she is."

He didn't like her tone. It insinuated that he'd been caught doing something he shouldn't have. "I've already said so. And what if I have heard of Megan Maitland? It doesn't change anything in my life."

That was just the point behind this reunion. "It might if you let it."

"Why?" he asked with a sneer, shifting Bethany to his other side. It was getting late and he had to get her to bed. "Is 'Aunt' Megan going to adopt me?"

He knew it was counterproductive to his cause to assume the attitude he was taking, but he couldn't help feeling somewhat contemptuous of the aunt who was summoning him now like a queen summoning some poor relation or peasant. What was her angle? In the world he'd grown up in, everyone had always had an angle or was looking to skim something off the top. His father had taught him that by word and example.

Maybe it was her imagination, but Greer thought she detected just a strain of hurt beneath the contempt. It surprised her that Rafe and she could actually relate on some level. She knew all about being ignored.

"No, but your aunt will make you feel as if you're a part of something if you let her."

It occurred to Greer that the odds were more than likely that Rafe didn't know he had a half brother and half sister, R.J. and Anna, the children his father had abandoned when his first wife had unexpectedly died in a car accident. Robert Maitland had left the two without any provision for their care. It was Megan and her husband William, Rafe's uncle, who had taken the children in and eventually adopted them.

It was on the tip of Greer's tongue to tell him about them and Mrs. Maitland's largesse, but then she stopped herself. Maybe telling him was something Mrs. Maitland wanted to handle on her own.

So, instead, Greer gave him a tiny peek into her own world. "That's what she did with me."

He wondered how much his aunt was paying this woman to sing her praises this way. "Oh, so now you're part of the family, too?"

Taking offense at the sarcasm wasn't going to accomplish anything, Greer told herself, so she ignored it.

"In a manner of speaking. Mrs. Maitland makes everyone feel at home, as if they've always been part of her world." She knew how surprised she'd been that first day, when Megan had walked into her office and greeted her as if she were an old friend. Working with Mrs. Maitland had done nothing to diminish her enthusiasm for the woman. But Greer was also aware of the danger of overselling. "Look, you're not going to be convinced until you meet her yourself and talk with her."

Maybe it was the long day, or the fact that his shoulder was aching, but Rafe simply didn't have any patience with rehashing this a second time. "I already said I was going…"

The look in his eyes was intimidating. Ordinarily, if she were speaking to him on her own behalf, Greer would have backed away long ago. But this was her job and she took anything associated with work very seriously. She reminded herself that that was what had almost caused her to have a nervous

breakdown on her last job. Taking everything so
seriously. Working as Mrs. Maitland's assistant was
supposed to be a walk in the park.

Looking into Rafe's eyes, she found that the
park's path had temporarily and ominously gotten
swallowed up in darkness.

She stuck it out. "Yes, but I want you to give
her a chance. Leave any prejudices behind and
judge her fairly."

Rafe studied her for a minute. There had to be
more than just her salary involved here. He wanted
to know what. "What does it matter to you? Is there
some kind of bonus for you for every breathing
body you bring back to the fold?"

"No, there's no bonus." She banked down the
disgust she felt at the suggestion. Was everything
about money to this man? "It matters to me because Mrs. Maitland is the most decent person I've
ever met and I don't want to see her hurt."

Maybe she was on the level at that, he mused.
"I don't intend to hurt her, Greer. Hell, I'll even
salute her if she wants."

She took the comment at face value. "A simple
hug would be more appreciated."

He wasn't a hugger or a toucher, for that matter.
There'd been no outward signs of affection in the
house he'd grown up in, no casual pats or enthu-
siastic embraces. Just six people caged in one cell,

marking time and looking to break free. Each one of them, except for Janelle, had struck out on their own the moment they legally could. Janelle had been the only one to celebrate her nineteenth birthday at home, but he'd be willing to make book that it hadn't been out of any sort of filial loyalty.

"Yeah, well, we'll see about that." She'd said something about leaving now. Had that been on the level or an exaggeration? "How soon is my presence requested?"

She knew Mrs. Maitland was anxious to meet with him. "As soon as you can get away."

Rafe paused, thinking as Bethany began to doze against his chest. Except for occasional days like today, it was the slow season at the ranch and he had more than enough vacation time accrued, never having taken more than a few days off in the last five years. There'd never been any real reason to until now.

"I'll talk to the boss," he promised, lowering his voice so as not to disturb Bethany. "Where can I get in touch with you? I'm assuming you're not going back to Austin until you have my head in your trophy bag."

"Your head won't do me much good without the rest of you," she informed him crisply. She'd gotten him to say yes, why wasn't the tension in her body leaving? "I'm staying at the Chamberlain Ho-

tel.'' The accommodations were spartan and limited, but clean, which was all she required. Living
the corporate high life had gotten her better rooms,
but had made antacids a permanent part of her daily
diet. ''Room 503.''

He made a mental note of the name and number.
''All right. I'll call you once I get the details ironed
out.''

With that, she found herself being ushered out
the front door.

She didn't bother with the hot shower she'd
promised herself, and put off ordering from room
service until she'd put in the all-important call to
her employer.

Slipping her shoes off, Greer rubbed her feet as
she listened to the ringing of the phone on the other
end. Mrs. Maitland had given her the number to her
home phone, telling her to call any time she had
news.

It pleased Greer to have news.

''Hello?''

Greer recognized Megan's voice immediately.
Soft, but with an unmistakable authoritative ring.

''Mrs. Maitland, this is Greer. Your nephew will
be happy to come to the reunion. He has to see to
a few things first. Once they're taken care of, he'll

be returning with me to Austin.'' She bit her lower lip, then added, ''He's excited about meeting you.''

All right, so it was a lie, but what did it hurt to make Mrs. Maitland feel as if Rafe cared about discovering a lost branch of the family? Greer argued with her conscience. There was no doubt in her mind that once he met the woman, Rafe Maitland would be singularly impressed with his aunt.

Megan's warm laugh filled the telephone receiver. ''Wonderful. I knew I could count on you, Greer. I hope it wasn't too difficult for you.''

Greer knew what Megan was referring to. She'd heard that the matriarch and her family had had dealings with Rafe's older sister, Janelle. All that had taken place before she'd come to work for Mrs. Maitland, but according to some people who were in a position to know, Rafe's sister had caused a great deal of damage. She'd kidnapped Megan's grandson and had her own husband pose as Megan's long lost firstborn, Connor, to try to swindle her out of some of her fortune. It was only natural for Megan to be concerned about what the other members of that branch of the family might be like. But it was a testimony to her large heart that she was willing to give them all a chance, anyway.

Provided Greer could locate Luke and Laura.

Well, she'd succeeded in locating Rafe, all right. Big time. Greer looked down at the ring on her finger. No matter how she moved it, it caught the light, scattering it into warm rainbows. Hypnotizing her.

"No, no trouble," she murmured.

The knots in her stomach refused to loosen, even though she was alone in her room. Thinking of Rafe Maitland only succeeded in tightening them.

Chapter 4

Megan replaced the receiver in the telephone cradle on the table beside her and smiled to herself.

It was going well.

She'd been right to give the assignment to Greer, even though the young woman had only been with her for a short while. Greer Lawford was a rare gem, loyal, dedicated and resourceful. And, from all appearances, selfless. Megan hoped it was true. The incident with Janelle and the treachery that had almost been the undoing of them all had temporarily shaken Megan's faith in her ability to read people.

Megan shrugged the thought away. Other than

her near-fatal error with Janelle, she'd generally had a knack for trusting the right people.

Except for one other time.

A distant sadness traced its spidery fingertips over her as she remembered. Megan shook her head. That had been a devastating mistake, too. But at seventeen she'd been starry-eyed, young and foolish, certainly not the woman she was today. And, she supposed, that mistake had served its purpose. It had laid the foundation of the person she was to become.

Why was she even thinking about that long-ago, ill-fated romance at a time like this? Everything was going well in her life. All her children were close by, happy and beginning families of their own. The clinic was thriving and she was mending long broken fences by bringing Janelle's siblings into the fold. This wasn't a time for sad thoughts, only happy ones.

Rising from her chair, Megan deliberately redirected her mood. She crossed to the wall of fine, old leather-bound books behind her. The house was quiet, the noise and myriad details of the day behind her, and she felt like reading something entertaining tonight. Something not too taxing.

Perhaps a mystery, she mused, drifting over to another section of the bookcase that contained more current, popular reading material.

She didn't hear the light rap on the door until it was followed by a louder knock. Turning around to glance over her shoulder, she saw the tall, thin figure standing in the doorway. Harold.

In the family's employ for more than four decades, the man still stood like a freshly minted West Point cadet, she thought with a smile. Over the years, she'd come to think of him more as an eccentric old uncle than her butler.

He cleared his throat politely. "I'm sorry to be intruding, Mrs. Maitland."

"You never intrude, Harold, you're as much a part of this old place as I am." She noted that the man's sallow face appeared to be more somber than usual. "Is there something wrong?" That was the trouble with paradise, William had once told her. Every so often, serpents appeared at the gate, looking to get in. She would have thought that, at least for this year, they'd seen their quota of snakes.

"There's someone to see you, ma'am."

She couldn't gauge from the old man's tone whether she would welcome her visitor or not. "Who is it?"

Harold squared his shoulders. "He wouldn't say, ma'am."

Harold never forgot the face of anyone who entered the house, so this had to be someone new. Yet there was something in his tone that felt disturbing.

Only one way to find out. So much for snatching a little private time, she thought, looking wistfully at the books to her left.

It suddenly occurred to her that whoever was looking for admittance might be embarrassed about giving their name. That was often the case with the young girls who sought her out here. They came to the house because they wanted to enter the clinic but had no money and thought that if they appealed to her privately, she wouldn't turn them away.

You'd think by now that everyone would know that no one was ever turned away from Maitland Maternity, Megan thought. That was why the clinic existed in the first place, to give troubled girls a place to go. That it had eventually turned out to be a trendy place where celebrities came to have their babies was just a whimsical, fortuitous turn of fate. The celebrity patients enabled the clinic to treat the girls who couldn't pay.

"Show the mystery person in," she told Harold.

She could see that he didn't appear happy about the instruction. Harold thought she was much too lax about her personal security.

As might be expected, his next words were "Perhaps you'd like me to call Mr. Blake." Hugh Blake was the steadfast family lawyer and lifelong friend she had come to treasure.

"Why?" Her mouth turned up humorously. "Am I being sued?"

Harold looked appalled at the very suggestion. "No, ma'am, but—"

She was quick to end his discomfort. "Show whoever it is in, Harold. I don't need a white knight standing by my side every time someone comes to call." That was the way she'd begun to think of Hugh lately, as a white knight ready to defend her at the slightest hint of trouble. She had to admit that she did rather like the idea. "And if I do, I'll call you," she promised gently.

Harold seemed to grow an inch before her. "Very well, ma'am."

Such a funny little man, she mused as he withdrew from the room. She turned back to her search for a book to read. Funny, but highly indispensable. She didn't know where they would have been without Harold all these years.

"Hello, Megan."

The moment before she heard him, she'd felt that something within the room had suddenly changed. The air, her surroundings, something.

When he spoke, it was to nudge forth a memory buried deep in the distant past.

Turning around, Megan was hardly conscious of breathing. There, just several feet away from her, was someone who suddenly erased more than forty-six years from her life in a heartbeat. Erased it and turned her into a flustered, seventeen-year-old girl on the brink of womanhood. Womanhood she had explored so willingly with him.

Clyde.

Clyde Mitchum.

The man who had left her pregnant and alone so many years ago. Connor's father. Older, yes, but it was still unmistakably him. She would have recognized Clyde anywhere.

She'd thought he was dead.

The book Megan was holding slipped from her numbed fingers.

He was quick to eliminate the space between them. Kneeling before her, he quickly picked up the book. She found her heart lodged in her throat as he rose before her, his eyes keen as they delved into hers. As if in slow motion, the book was returned to her hand.

"It's been a long time," he said softly. "And you're even more beautiful than I remembered you."

Sand seemed to fill her mouth as she searched for her tongue. "What are you doing here?"

"That's easy." His tone was low. Contrite. "I've come to beg your forgiveness."

Megan felt as if her whole world had suddenly been upended.

* * *

"So this is the famous Maitland estate," Rafe muttered two days later, more to himself and the baby he'd just extricated from the hastily purchased car seat than to the woman who was getting out of the driver's side of the car and coming toward him.

It wasn't what he'd anticipated.

Being raised in Las Vegas, he'd come to expect most things to be bigger than life, especially when those things belonged to people who had more money than God. Granted, the three-story building he was looking at was large, but it was also in good taste, something his mother with her showgirl background had only aspired to but never mastered.

As they had been approaching on the driveway, Rafe had noted that the main house had a smaller building to the rear of it. Probably had made it easier for the old man when he was alive to sneak away and have his trysts, Rafe mused. His own old man hadn't had the decency even to try to maintain a facade and hide his affairs. The last straw, he'd been told, had been when his mother had caught his father with a much younger woman in their bed one afternoon when she'd come home too early. Rafe had gathered that the indiscretion hadn't been the first, but this time his mother had sent his father packing.

All things considered, Rafe didn't think much of

the institution of marriage. Except for Lil and Rory, he'd never come across a couple who wouldn't have been happier apart than together.

Greer shut the door and realized she was clutching her keys too hard. "This is it," she affirmed.

She had no idea why she was feeling so nervous about his meeting Mrs. Maitland. You would have thought she was the one who was meeting a long lost member of her family, not Rafe. But for her, that would have been impossible. Her own people were dead now. That much she knew. She'd hired a private investigator to find her parents with the first money she'd earned after graduating from college. It had been her gift to herself. Not that there had been anyone else to give her anything other than the diploma she'd worked so hard to earn.

The experience of having someone go out of their way to find her and bring her into their family was one she would have dearly loved. She wondered if Rafe appreciated how lucky he was.

Glancing at his expression now, Greer rather doubted it.

Rafe waited for her to round the hood of the car and join him. When she did, he looked at her significantly. "Ready?"

It seemed an odd thing for him to say. "Shouldn't I be the one asking you that? After all, she is your aunt.'' Bethany's sweater had slipped off one shoulder and Greer adjusted it as she talked.

Rafe frowned slightly. Megan Maitland was a stranger whether or not he knew her name and regardless of the blood flowing through her veins. All that mattered to him about the woman was that she ultimately agree to back him up when the time came.

He'd worked out the details in his mind last night. He'd put in a couple of weeks visiting this society maven who'd suddenly become so family oriented, then return to talk to his lawyer about the unexpected change in his circumstances. Acquiring a fiancée and having his connection to the Maitlands come to light could only work in his favor. He was willing to give Megan Maitland every Christmas between now and eternity if it meant he could keep Bethany.

In response to Greer's question, he looked down at her left hand.

''Oh, right, that.'' How could she have forgotten about that? The weight of the ring acted as a constant reminder. It weighed even more heavily on her conscience. ''Um, I thought maybe I'd hold off telling her about that for a while.''

About to walk up to the front door, he stopped. ''I'm no expert, but isn't a woman usually excited when she gets engaged for the first time? Wouldn't that mean that she'd want everyone to know she was engaged and not hide the fact?''

She looked at him in surprise. Did it actually show, or was he just making a logical assumption? "How did you know I was never engaged?"

It was a hunch, but he figured a safe one. "Just a guess," he told her, doing his best to sound genial. Hurting her feelings, or worse, insulting her, might make her decide not to go through with this now that she had him here. He couldn't take that chance.

"You're right," she muttered. When he looked at her, raising a brow, she added, "About both things."

"I've never been engaged, either," he told her, his voice kind.

The revelation made her look at him in surprise. Not that he hadn't been engaged, but that he'd sounded kind when he said it. He didn't sound as if he was talking down to her or having fun at her expense. Given who and what he was, a man who had been around the block more than once, she would have expected him to be more abrupt or at the very least, insensitive.

The next moment, he took her hand. Her pulse jumped.

She looked skittish again, he thought. Like a horse that needed a firm, gentle hand to keep it in line. It was something he was good at, though he normally didn't exercise that knack with people. "Newly engaged people tend to hold hands."

She forced herself to ignore the army of tiny ants that were suddenly rushing up and down the length of her arm in response to his touch.

"If you say so," she murmured under her breath. Her hand in his, she walked up to the front door and rang the bell.

His black livery made the tall, aged butler appear even thinner than he was as he offered Greer a wispy smile in greeting before scrutinizing the man at her side when he opened the door.

Like a diver about to jump off the high board, Greer took a deep breath before venturing to say a word. "Hello, Harold, Mrs. Maitland is expecting us."

Harold didn't appear to be completely convinced about the "us" part, but he stepped aside as he opened the front door farther. Once they were inside, he shut it firmly behind them.

"If you'll wait right here, I'll announce you." It was not a request but an instruction.

Rafe watched the man disappear down the marble-tiled floors and snorted at the idea of needing to be announced. Most of the people he knew could see from one end of their house to the other in one sweeping glance. There was no need to be announced by anyone.

He felt Greer's fingers tense in his. You would have thought she was the one being looked over, not him.

Still holding her hand, he looked at her. She had skin like snow. Even so, it seemed a shade lighter. "What's the matter?"

Nervous, she ran the tip of her tongue along her lips. It didn't help. "As you pointed out, I've never been engaged before."

"Engaged? Greer, when?"

They both turned to see Megan Maitland sweep into the foyer. Within an instant, the surprised look on her face gave way to a wide smile that lit up her entire face. She took both of Greer's hands in hers as if she were greeting her daughter, not her employee.

"Darling, how wonderful for you. But who? When? You never told me there was anyone special."

Guilt stabbed at Greer's chest repeatedly, making it difficult to breathe evenly.

Don't stutter, don't stutter, Greer cautioned herself, afraid she would revert to an old childhood habit it had taken her years to conquer.

"There is," she answered evenly. "Him." Her

lips pressed together in a tight smile, she indicated Rafe with her eyes.

Megan's smile was warm and encompassing as it took him in. She put her hand out. "Hello, I'm Megan Maitland. I'm sorry, you caught me off guard. I was expecting to meet my nephew, not Greer's intended..."

Like the house, the woman was not what he expected. There were no jewels dripping from her wrists, neck and ears, no blinding rings on her hands. There was nothing ostentatious about her. She had skin almost like a young girl's, though he knew she had to be in her early sixties. She was dressed in a conservative skirt and blouse, not the flowing caftans his mother used to favor when she stayed at home.

Because he found the smile disarming and engaging, he looked into Megan's eyes.

"I'm both," Rafe replied, taking the hand that the woman extended toward him. To his amusement, he saw surprise flash in her eyes. The next moment, it subsided. She impressed him with her control.

"Oh." She looked at the younger woman. "Greer, I know I told you to use any means available to get Rafe to come here, but I meant within reason. I certainly didn't mean for you to propose to him."

Flustered, Greer missed the teasing note in Megan's voice. All she heard was the concern. "I didn't, that is—"

"I proposed to her," Rafe corrected, cutting in.

Megan wasn't sure what to make of any of this. For the time being, she didn't allow her attention to be diverted to the baby he was holding. That there was one only added to the confusion. "I thought you said you didn't know him."

"I didn't—" Greer caught her lower lip between her teeth. How should she put this? A masters in English as well as business, thousands of words at her disposal and she couldn't glue three together to form a successful, convincing lie. "What I mean is—"

Lying had been a way of life in the world Rafe had once lived in. Lies came easily to him, though he was no longer in the habit of falling back on them.

"It was one of those love-at-first-sight things," Rafe told Megan, slipping his free hand around Greer's waist and drawing her closer to him. "I'm the kind of man who knows what he wants when he sees it, and what I saw was quality." Even as he said it, he brushed Greer's cheek with a kiss.

At least, that had been his intention. Startled, Greer abruptly turned her head and his lips made contact with hers. That it wasn't an unpleasant sensation, or even at best, a neutral one, surprised him. It surprised him even more that there had been a fleeting feeling of a fuse being lit within him. But the next second, it was gone.

The smile that came to his lips was an afterthought.

Startled, Greer did her best to hide her surprise. She wondered if anyone besides her noticed that her pulse had just broken the sound barrier. She took in a deep, shaky breath.

Megan watched the two younger people before her thoughtfully. There was definitely something going on. Something beyond the apparent. She would have thought that a quickly struck match was the last thing to have occurred in either of their lives.

"I see. Well, I won't pretend to say I understand, exactly, but I am happy for you. Provided you are happy." She looked at Greer, waiting for the younger woman to either confirm or deny the statement.

That was her cue, Greer realized. "Oh, yes, very happy." She slipped her arm through Rafe's in a move that was a little less than smooth. "M—Rafe—" she'd almost slipped and said Mr. Maitland "—is everything I've ever wanted in a man."

Megan could readily believe that. Rafe Maitland was as good-looking as they came. There was a lot about this long lost nephew of hers that reminded her of William when he was a young man. Rafe had the same rugged good looks, the same independent air. But she didn't quite understand what a man who looked like that would see in Greer on such short notice. That Greer was a rare woman was not in question, but it took time to perceive this, and these young people had known each other, what, perhaps two days? Forty-eight hours was an incredibly short time in which to make a life-altering decision.

Her own thought mocked her. How long had it taken her to believe that her life was meant to be spent with Clyde?

A day? Three?

But Greer was a successful thirty-year-old businesswoman, not a naive, impressionable child, and Rafe was five years her junior, if she wasn't mistaken. It didn't make any sense to her.

Still, he had referred to Greer as a woman of quality. Maybe he did know her, after all...

Megan studied her nephew closely as she asked, ''And is Greer everything you've ever wanted in a woman, Rafe?''

He knew if he replied too enthusiastically, the woman would smell a rat. One look into her eyes told him she was one shrewd cookie who didn't let others do her thinking for her. He was going to have to be honest whenever possible. He didn't want anything to spoil this.

"Pretty close," he replied. And then he looked at Greer. The imprint of her hesitant mouth was still fresh on his. It stirred something sweet within him. "I certainly couldn't ask for a better one."

Well, maybe there was more to this than she thought, Megan mused. Maybe Rafe was a great deal sharper than his father had been when it came to judging character and net worth. As she remembered, Robert Sr. had been hopelessly shallow.

"Well, you certainly have that right," Megan replied with enthusiasm. She saw color creep up Greer's cheeks. For the time being, she was going to let things float along and see where they went. "Well, it seems that not only am I going to have to throw you a welcome-to-the-fold dinner—" she turned from Rafe and looked at Greer, "—but a welcome-to-the-family one for you as well."

Megan welcomed the diversion after Clyde's surprise visit two nights ago. Clyde had stayed only a little while, saying that he'd returned after all this time to try to make amends. He'd sworn to her that he was a changed man and wanted nothing more than the opportunity to prove that to her. He'd also wanted to meet their son. She'd sent Clyde away, saying that she needed time to think about it.

She would rather think about the couple in front of her.

Guilt started churning again in full force. Greer slanted a side glance at Rafe. She really didn't feel right about lying to Mrs. Maitland like this. But one look at Rafe's face banished almost all of her qualms. He was looking at her the way a man looked at the woman he cared about.

Her heart quickened as she slid her tongue along her lips again. She could taste him. Greer found she was having difficulty breathing.

"Please don't trouble yourself on my account, Mrs. Maitland."

"You'll find that Greer is very unassuming," Megan told Rafe as if in confidence.

That out of the way for the time being, she turned her attention to the baby he was holding. Even as she did, her heart swelled. "And who is this precious darling?"

Stretching her arms out to Bethany, she was pleased when the little girl came to her without hesitation. Megan cuddled the toddler against her, murmuring a few words of endearment to her. There was nothing she loved more than holding a baby in her arms. It brought back so many memories, flooded her with so much positive energy and hope.

Stroking the little girl's silky dark hair, Megan

looked at Rafe for an explanation. "I didn't realize you had a daughter."

Here the truth was definitely appropriate and could only further his case for him. "She belonged to some friends of mine who were killed in a car accident last month."

And he was taking care of her, Megan thought. That spoke well of him. It reminded her of what William had done when confronted with his brother's abandoned children. Maybe Rafe was more like his uncle than his father. It was a heartening thought.

"Come into the living room, both of you," Megan requested, turning to lead the way. "There's a great deal to talk about."

Greer glanced at Rafe before falling into step behind Megan. Yes, she thought, there was. She only hoped she'd be able to say the right thing. Being too close to Rafe was definitely beginning to scramble her thoughts.

Chapter 5

Megan sat down on the far end of the sofa, placing Bethany on her lap with the unselfconscious ease of a woman who had been around babies for most of her life. She gestured towards the comfortable, butter-soft leather sofa, waiting for Greer and Rafe to sit down beside her.

"So tell me about this whirlwind courtship of yours." Smiling expectantly, she looked from Rafe to Greer, leaving the floor open for either one of them to jump in and begin.

Mentally, Greer shut her eyes and pretended she was addressing the chairman of the board with a progress report. Experience told her that to approach the situation in any other fashion would only trip her up. Wrapping herself up in a persona she had created for career purposes was the only way she could summon the lies that were needed to keep this charade going.

Composed, she spared only a glance toward Rafe before looking at her employer.

"Actually, it isn't as whirlwind as you might think, Mrs. Maitland. It turns out that I actually knew Rafe from high school."

To Rafe's credit, he didn't turn suddenly to look at her, but she could feel just the slightest shift on the sofa beside her to indicate his surprise at this new fabrication out of the clear blue.

Megan tilted her head as she looked from the baby on her lap to Greer. "But I thought you said you were an orphan."

Greer smiled as if she were slightly amused at the other woman's confusion. "Even orphans go to school, Mrs. Maitland."

"Yes, of course, I didn't mean that the way it sounded." Megan backed away, not wanting to give offense. "I mean, I thought you said you were raised in different foster homes throughout Texas, so naturally I'm a little surprised that you would know Rafe, since as far as I know he spent the first part of his life in Las Vegas." Megan's eyes shifted toward her nephew, wondering if there was to be any sort of contradiction forthcoming. There wasn't.

The memory had come to her aid out of the blue. Greer hadn't thought of the Wendells in years. "One of the families I lived with had to relocate temporarily to Las Vegas—the father was in construction and his company had a contract for some work on one of the new casinos that were going up." With effort, she tried to put on her most smitten expression, hoping her nerves wouldn't give her away. Greer slipped her hand over Rafe's as she looked at him adoringly. "We had a summer romance when I was sixteen."

The words struck a chord. "Almost as old as I was—" Megan stopped abruptly.

Wrapped up in the charade, and in the way touching Rafe felt, Greer heard only the murmur of Megan's voice, not any of the words.

"Excuse me?"

Slightly flustered, Megan roused herself. Silly the way this mood kept trying to take hold of her, reducing her to a teenage girl when she was decades beyond that. "Oh, nothing. Sorry, just reminiscing for a moment."

But it was far more than that, unfortunately. Clyde's sudden return had turned everything upside down in her world. As had his declaration that he wanted to make things up to her and was willing to do anything to prove that he was a changed man. He claimed that he now knew he should never have left her, but he'd been little more than a frightened boy himself and unable to shoulder the responsibility of being a father.

The years had ultimately been kind to her, but Megan was a great deal more suspicious now than she had been when she had last seen Clyde. Still, there was no denying that there were residual feelings to sort through and deal with, feelings she could have sworn had disappeared after all these years. Feelings that belonged to the girl she had once been.

Megan forced herself to focus on the moment and on statements that clearly didn't hold water. Her expression remained warm and friendly as she asked, "So when I asked you to locate him for me, didn't his name ring a bell?"

It wasn't hard for Greer to dig a little to bring out feelings that had been very much a part of her life in her formative years.

"Quite frankly, no. Back then, last names never mattered to me. I didn't have one so everyone else's really didn't register." It had been a defense mechanism she'd used to make herself feel better. "It made me more like other people."

Greer was aware that Rafe was now looking at her intently, but she was afraid that if she glanced in his direction, she might lose her nerve or, at the very least, her train of thought. He had very penetrating green eyes that did unfortunate things to her brain.

For the most part, what she was telling Megan was true. There had been a family that had temporarily moved to Las Vegas and she had spent the summer there, but there had been no summer romance with anyone, at least, not for her. That had been experienced by Rachel, the Wendells' oldest daughter. The one who had looked like a beauty contest winner at sixteen. The extent of her own part in the summer romance was to serve as a convenient cover for Rachel. They'd tell Rachel's parents that they were going out together and then Rachel would dash off to see her boyfriend, a blackjack dealer at one of the casinos, as soon as it was safe. She was always left behind to spend the day alone and to look on wistfully, wondering when her time would come.

And if it would come.

Moved by the story, knowing what it felt like to be both on the outside and left behind after a summer romance, Megan reached over and squeezed Greer's hand. The look that passed between them was one of silent camaraderie.

Greer managed to keep the guilt from registering on her face, but it wasn't easy.

Straightening, Megan looked at the little girl on her lap.

"Well, I have a great many more questions and a lot of catching up to do with you," she told Rafe, "but this little one looks very tired." She rose to her feet with Bethany in her arms. "Why don't you put her down for a nap and get freshened up first?"

Rafe had risen with his aunt, surprised that she appeared so easygoing. But his suspicions wouldn't dissipate easily. He figured the telling word here was *appeared*.

"Sounds like a plan to me." He took Bethany from her. Making a noise, Bethany curled against him as if he was a favored toy that made her feel secure. Her eyes closed almost immediately. Rafe lowered his voice. "Where will we be staying?"

It looked as if this time the apple had fallen a great distance from the tree, Megan thought. A great many men naturally assumed that a baby was the domain of any female within calling range. Unlike his late father, Rafe seemed to take on the responsibility of caring for the little girl as if it were second nature to him.

She took an instant liking to her newly discovered nephew.

Megan walked with them to the front door. "I thought you might like to stay at the guesthouse." She turned to the woman who had become so invaluable to her in the last few months. Looking at Greer, Megan would have thought that love would have a difficult time finding a place in the young woman's life. She was happy that she was wrong. "Greer, you know where it is. I leave settling your new fiancé in in your capable hands." She glanced at her watch more out of habit than need. Megan prided herself on instinctively remaining on schedule. "I have to be getting to the clinic, but dinner is in your honor tonight and I'd like you both to attend." She looked at Greer warmly.

Greer knew she looked uncomfortable before she could catch herself and bank down the emotion. "Of course. Thank you, Mrs. Maitland."

"No," Megan corrected her, leaning over and brushing a kiss on the young woman's cheek. "Thank *you*."

Saying goodbye, Megan watched them thoughtfully as they walked around to the rear of the property.

"You know, looks are deceiving."

Leading the way to the guesthouse, which stood in the shadow of the main building, Greer glanced back at Rafe. She thought he was talking about Megan. Protective instincts immediately rose to the fore. "What are you referring to?"

He lengthened his stride a touch and was next to

her in one beat. His eyes looked straight into her soul. "You."

His answer caught her completely off guard. "What?" Greer scrambled for composure. "I mean, what makes you say that?"

He had to admit he kind of liked the way she was continually getting flustered around him and then trying desperately to exercise some kind of control over herself. He found himself idly wondering if she got that flustered when someone kissed her.

Probably, he decided. It surprised him that a small part of him wanted to conduct the experiment to find out firsthand.

"Well, looking at you I would have never thought you were such an accomplished little liar."

Her heel caught and wedged itself in a crack along the tiled walkway and she would have tripped had he not quickly caught her arm.

"Hey, I didn't mean for you—"

She flushed, waving away the apology before it was completed. Regaining some of her composure, she pulled herself together.

"It wasn't a complete lie," she said, avoiding his eyes as she continued to lead the way to the guesthouse. "There was a family that relocated to Las Vegas for the summer. Actually, for seven months." She remembered how bitterly the children had complained about having to uproot and go to school in a different place. For her, it had been a way of life, something she had long since stopped resisting. "And I did live with them during that time."

Leaning slightly forward, Rafe tried to catch a glimpse of her face rather than just her profile. "And was there a romance?"

"Yes," she retorted, then relented. If she started lying to Rafe as well, it would be incredibly difficult to keep all her stories straight. She could deal with omissions, but not wanton fabrications. "But not mine."

He heard the wistfulnes in her voice and realized that he felt sorry for her. She was probably overlooked all the time. Part of it, he figured, was her fault. After all, look at the way the woman dressed, like someone twenty years older than her age. That wasn't something that just happened overnight.

Rafe thought better of voicing his observations. Instead, he nodded at her as she unlocked the door to the guesthouse. "Very resourceful."

She shrugged, not looking at him as she led the way inside the cheery one-story building. Waiting, Greer closed the door behind them after Rafe crossed the threshold. "I made a bargain with you. I intend to keep my part of it."

Rafe glanced around. Like the main house, the

guesthouse was decorated with a sparing, tasteful hand. He figured whoever did it had to be a man. The place lacked frills. "I'm impressed."

She wasn't sure if she was being complimented or mocked. On the whole, Rafe Maitland wasn't an easy man to read. "Why? Because I keep my word?"

"Because you're quicker than I gave you credit for." She was. His first impression, that she was a skittish colt, seemed at least partially unjustified. "I admire someone who knows how to think on her feet." He watched for a second as pink climbed up the side of her neck. Woman had to learn how to take a compliment, he thought. He changed his tone, distancing himself from her as he looked around the rest of the guesthouse. "Practically speaking, if the judge questions you, I think you'll do fine."

Embarrassed, Greer realized she hadn't really given much thought to that yet. Getting him here had taken all her attention. But there was a piper to pay and she knew she had to start thinking about that. More things on her list of things to do, she thought, trying not to feel swamped.

"Maybe we should get our stories straight, then."

"Good idea." He nodded, crossing back to her. "Why did you tell her that you knew me before?"

She wished he'd stop looking at her like that. She liked it a lot better when he was looking somewhere else. It gave her stomach a fighting chance to settle down. You'd think she was some kind of silly schoolgirl, she upbraided herself, instead of a woman talking to a man five years her junior.

Five years separated them, she thought suddenly. Five years and an entire galaxy. He was a Maitland, after all, and she was just a question mark. A question mark whose parents hadn't wanted any part of her.

Greer summoned her best detached, corporate manner. "Because Mrs. Maitland's a very shrewd judge of character. She knows I'm not the type to fall head over heels for someone in a matter of a few hours."

He wasn't as convinced about that as she apparently was. There was something in her eyes that told him Greer Lawford might very well do that cartwheel into romance that she was so scornful of.

"And what type are you?" he asked, his voice dropping low.

She knew he was speaking so softly because he didn't want to wake the little girl in his arms, but it really unnerved her; his voice seemed to creep in right under her skin and caress the very core of her.

She tried to think about something else. "The type who measures twice before she cuts once."

He smiled, amused at the utilitarian comparison. "Like a carpenter."

Her eyes held his as she tried to maintain her ground. "Like a cautious person." Then, turning on her heel, Greer led the way to the back. There were two bedrooms in the guesthouse. She was going to have to see about getting a crib brought into this one.

Rafe carefully placed Bethany in the center of the bed, then began dragging over the armchair that was in the corner of the room. It wasn't going to be enough to form a barricade. They'd passed a small kitchen on their way to the bedroom.

"Watch her while I get some chairs," he told Greer as he walked out.

He brought all four chairs, two at a time, into the room, surrounding the bed so that Bethany wouldn't roll over and fall off.

"I'll have a crib brought in," Greer promised.

He nodded at the information. "Won't keep her from falling off now, though, will it?"

"No," she murmured, beginning to leave.

"Was she right?"

The softly spoken question stopped her. At the doorway, Greer turned around to look at Rafe and was surprised to find that he was beside her. It took her a second to get her bearings.

"About what?"

"About you being an orphan?"

She hated that word. Hated it because it had haunted her for most of her childhood and adolescence. Hated it because it made her feel so lonely. "My past isn't part of the bargain."

"It is if the judge asks." That, he told himself, was the only reason he was asking her personal questions. But if he were being truthful with himself, he would have admitted that a part of him was curious about this strange lady that fate had thrown his way. "All I'm asking for is the same information you've obviously already given my aunt—provided you weren't being resourceful at that time, too."

Greer took offense. He thought she'd lied to Megan.

Well, why wouldn't he? She was lying now, wasn't she? What else would he think? She hated this netherworld she was suddenly in, all for the best of reasons.

"There was no need to be. And I told her in a moment of confidence because I both like and respect your aunt." She tried to look as indignant as possible. "When I can say the same for you, I'll tell you."

For the first time since she had met him, he laughed. The sound was deep, resonant and went right into her bones like a well-aimed arrow. Greer could feel something stirring inside her, a tantalizing yearning that took her completely by surprise.

"You're a feisty one, Greer." There was a touch of admiration in his eyes as he looked at her. "A lot more feisty than I first thought."

She knew she shouldn't be reacting to this as if it were a compliment, but she couldn't seem to stop herself. "That would be because you were judging a book by its cover." And she knew full well what her "cover" looked like. "A lot of people are guilty of that."

"A book, eh?" The laugh had subsided into a smile that was almost lethal. "Something tells me you're not the quick read I thought."

This was ridiculous. In another minute, she was going to be guilty of trapping herself in the scenario she'd outlined for Megan. Granted, the man brought new meaning to the word *sexy*, but sexy men were not in her realm of attainment and she knew that. If there was ever going to be a man in her life, he was going to be a male counterpart of her. Solid, steady and, most likely, another book whose cover people misread.

"No," she informed him, "I'm not. Now, is there anything else you need?"

He didn't need to pause to think. "Diapers and baby food."

She hadn't thought of that when she'd called last

night and left orders to stock the refrigerator. Just
like she'd overlooked the crib.

You're slipping, Greer.

"Right." She hated that he'd caught her in a slip-
up, though he didn't seem to be gloating. "I'll get
right on it."

Something within Rafe egged him on to tease
her, but that would have come under the heading
of "cruel," he decided. That skittishness he noticed
about her seemed to have returned in full bloom.
He could see it in her eyes as she reached the front
door.

So he remained where he was, letting her open
the door and make good her retreat.

"I'd appreciate it," he told her just before she
shut the door again.

"That is one odd lady," he murmured quietly to
himself, turning away.

Getting dressed up had always been against his
principles. He supposed that because both his parents set such store by outward appearance, he'd re-
belled against it. Given a choice, he much preferred
the freedom of jeans to the confinement of "monkey suits," which to him were not just tuxedos but
jackets and any trousers that required a crease in
them. He had found a suit jacket, trousers and
matching shirt laid out on his bed when he'd come

out of his shower this evening. Someone had come into the room while he was showering and left them for him.

He didn't know if he liked a place where people slipped in and out unannounced, leaving things in their wake. He was a man who valued his privacy above almost all else. To him it was far more precious than any silver that had once been mined in the fields that overlooked Virginia City.

Still, this was all about Bethany, not him. He couldn't expect Greer to live up to her part of the bargain if he didn't honor his. Besides, there was his aunt. Getting on her good side didn't seem like much of a trick and he could sure use her support when the time came. He had a hunch that it would handily tip the scales in his favor.

He was, to use his parents' vernacular, in a win-win situation. As long as he didn't blow it.

That obviously meant monkey suits, he thought, resigned. With a sigh, he donned the shirt, the pants and then the jacket. It didn't surprise him that they all fit as if they'd been made for him. It was in keeping with the efficiency of the place.

He eyed the tie that had been placed alongside the rest of the clothes. There was no way he was going to put it on no matter what was at stake. In his opinion, ties were too much like nooses, and he saw no point in wearing one.

The person who'd come in with his clothes had also put both diapers and a small pink-and-white dress for Bethany in what was to be the baby's room. He didn't bother opening the refrigerator. He just assumed that there was baby food on the shelves now. It seemed that his aunt thought of everything.

Either that, or her able-bodied assistant did.

His mouth curved slightly. Too bad Greer wasn't quite that—able bodied. Although, to be honest, he wasn't all that sure just what kind of body existed beneath her schoolmarmish clothes, other than thin.

He wondered what she'd wear to this mandated dinner party.

Shrugging, he dismissed the thought. Didn't matter to him what she wore or didn't wear. He just wanted all this to be over with. That included the family court hearing that was hanging over him. He shook his head. For a man who liked the simple life, things had gotten mighty complicated in the last month or so.

Bethany began kicking her feet, letting him know that she was awake with energy to spare. Time to get her dressed, he thought. "Hi there, sleepy-head," he said, leaning over to pick her up.

The knock he heard at the front door succeeded in irritating him. He had his hands full of baby and wasn't about to leave her to admit anyone. Whoever was on the other side of the door was just going to have to wait until he was finished.

The knock came again, this time a bit more loudly. "What?" he bit off, not expecting to be heard. "People can't seem to leave anyone alone around here," he said more to himself than to Bethany. The baby gurgled in response.

A minute later, he heard the door being opened and Greer calling out. "Hello? Are you in here?"

"In the back with Bethany," he responded, raising his voice. And then he lowered it again. "Talk about lack of privacy."

The next minute, Greer stuck her head in, her expression hesitant. "Hi, I just thought you might need some help."

Now that she offered, he could use some. Dressing Bethany in something other than practical rompers had proved to be a challenge. "How are you with frills?" he asked, without looking up.

Greer crossed to the bed. "Fair to middling."

"See if you can 'middle' this." Straightening, he gestured toward the small moving target on the bed. "I can't get the buttons closed. She's wiggling too much."

Greer caught her lower lip between her teeth, thinking of her first encounter with Bethany. But this didn't appear to require any holding, so maybe she was on safe ground this time.

"Put her on her tummy and you might have better luck."

He gestured toward the bed, taking a step back. "Feel free to have a go at it."

The instant he said it, Bethany rolled over onto her stomach and began to work her way up to the headboard—sideways. Greer made a lunge for her and caught the baby by the leg, keeping her from making good her escape.

"You're a regular wiggle worm, aren't you?" Gently, she brought Bethany back down, then, very methodically, she made quick work of the five buttons that had defied Rafe's fingers.

Standing back and watching, Rafe had his first opportunity to actually look at Greer. Like her other clothes, what she wore in the evening could be described as tailored and practical. She was wearing a long navy dress whose straight skirt fell to her mid-calf. It made him wonder if there were any curves at all beneath the material. So far, he hadn't been given a clue. Didn't all women have some kind of curves?

She could feel his eyes on her just by the way the room had begun to grow warmer. Straightening up, the baby in her arms, she turned to look at him. "What are you looking at?"

His eyes swept over her one last time before coming to rest on her face.

"Do you own anything that, you know, doesn't use up two bolts of material?"

Immediately self-conscious, Greer shifted the baby as if to use the small body as a shield. "I'm not sure I know what you're talking about." Her mouth felt dry. "I dress accordingly."

"According to what?" he couldn't help asking. "Camping Tents R Us?"

She could feel her face growing red. She didn't need this, didn't need to feel as though she were still the charity case left in the last pew of the church.

"Look, the bargain didn't include you insulting me." She thrust the baby at him.

Taking Bethany, he still managed to catch Greer's arm to keep her still. "I'm not trying to insult you, I'm just being curious. Don't you have something more, um—" Words had never been his long suit. "Girl-like?"

She blew out a breath. "I believe you're trying for the word *feminine.*"

He knew she was lashing out with a put-down, but the attempt was small potatoes. He'd certainly endured a great deal worse from his father.

"No, 'girl-like.' I figured you'd work your way up to feminine once you got the knack of it." He cocked his head. "You've got nice lines, woman. Don't be afraid to show them."

He was talking to her as if she were some kind of Thoroughbred. Well, she wasn't. She was the kind of animal that was hitched to a plow and got the job done. Still, she supposed that maybe he wasn't trying to be insulting. Horses were what he knew, she consoled herself.

"I'll take it under advisement," she murmured.

He bit back a laugh. She made everything sound as if it were going on in the boardroom. He began to really wonder about the woman he'd conned into this agreement. What was she like away from work? Did she know how to kick back, or were her nights only spaces of time she marked off while waiting to get back to work the next morning? He'd known a few people like that, people who had no lives except the one they'd hired onto.

"Thanks for the supplies," he said by way of making peace.

She nodded. "I'm glad the clothes fit."

He'd meant the food and diapers, not his clothes. "You sent them over?"

She nodded. "I didn't want you to feel out of place." That hadn't come out quite right, she realized. "Everyone dresses for a formal dinner," she explained.

She was looking out for him. He found that amusing. "Thanks."

How was it, he wondered, that this woman could

pick out a man's clothes, but hadn't a clue as to what was attractive when it came to her own way of dressing?

Or was it that she was purposely trying to maintain her plain appearance?

As he walked out of the guesthouse, Bethany in his arms, he realized that he was more than a little curious to find out the answer to that.

Chapter 6

Greer snuck a look in Rafe's direction, trying to gauge his reaction as he stood stoically beside her, holding Bethany in his arms, a few minutes later. At first glance, there appeared to be a sea of people within the room they'd just entered.

She knew how she'd feel, confronted with this many new faces, most of whom were related to her either directly or by marriage. Having a family—a real family, not one that would be gone at the end of the month, or three, or six because the county had found another place to deposit her temporarily—was something she'd always dreamed about. Greer knew that if she'd ever found herself in

Rafe's place, she would have been nervous about what they thought of her.

But one glance at Rafe's face told her that her reaction wasn't even remotely shared by him. Judging from his expression, all he appeared to have was a passingly mild interest in the people gathered.

Didn't meeting these people for the first time affect him? It was affecting her by proxy, she thought, and she wasn't even related to them.

Megan, wearing a soft blue dress that showed off the same graceful figure she'd had as a young girl, saw them first.

"You're here at last," she declared, delighted.

Conversation abruptly stopped within the room. Megan exchanged a few words with the distinguished-looking gentleman standing beside her, her long-time lawyer, friend and confidant, Hugh, before sailing across the room to them. She smiled at Greer before slipping her arm through Rafe's.

"Greer, I'm afraid I need to steal this handsome man away from you. But just for a moment." She winked. "I promise."

Megan sounded as if she were unofficially asking her permission. How odd was that? Greer thought, a sliver of pleasure wriggling through her. The older woman made it sound as if Rafe actually belonged to her.

As if anyone ever would, Greer thought with a sudden wave of regret that popped out of nowhere.

"Of course," she murmured, taking Bethany from Rafe before stepping back. He looked at her in surprise, then nodded his thanks. After a second, Bethany settled comfortably against her.

"They don't bite," Megan promised Rafe in a whisper before turning her face toward the gathering. "Everyone, this is Rafe, your cousin," she announced, looking from one group of young people to another, all of whom were completely unfamiliar to Rafe. But she meant to change that right now. "All except yours, of course," she added addressing the qualifying remark to the two couples who were off to the side of the room.

Rafe took it to mean that they weren't relations, or at the very least, that they belonged to another branch of the family that was separated from his by divorce, pestilence or whatever it was that severed family ties. He wondered just how long he would have to endure this evening before he could make his apologies and safely withdraw. He preferred his conversations one on one, or better yet, not at all.

His eyes swept over the gathering quickly. There were a great many people in the room, sixteen of Megan's children and their spouses if he didn't count his aunt and Greer. He realized that Megan still had her arm threaded through his and was gently but firmly steering him toward the foursome she'd singled out.

Megan took a deep breath before making the introductions, though she knew that on the part of her two oldest children, none was really necessary. They'd been eagerly awaiting this moment for some time now.

"R.J., Anna, this is your half brother, Rafe."

The boredom that had been hovering, waiting to overtake him, disappeared as surprise suddenly leaped into Rafe's veins.

"Hey, hold on a minute." Pulling his arm away from his aunt, he stepped back until he had all of them, including Megan, within his direct line of vision. He was only vaguely aware that Greer, still holding Bethany, had come to his side. "Just what the hell are you talking about?" he demanded, his eyes narrowing as he pinned Megan with a look.

"You didn't know?" Distress vibrated through the question as realization sank in. "Oh, Rafe, I'm so sorry. If I'd only known, I would have prepared you for this. I'd just assumed that you knew—"

Rafe still wasn't sure what his aunt was talking about. "That I knew what?"

Megan was aware that her children and Hugh were closing ranks around them, drawing as close physically as they did emotionally whenever there was a crisis. "That your father was married before."

Rafe took a deep breath before saying anything. He was obviously pulling himself together and regaining control, although Greer could see the muscle in his jaw still tensing.

"No, I didn't know he was married before. My father didn't exactly keep us in the loop about his life."

Now that he thought of it, Rafe realized that there had been hints dropped by his mother, though nothing had ever been specifically said about the existence of another wife. And certainly not about the existence of another family.

His eyes washed over first the man, then the woman. Rafe supposed he could see some resemblance to his father. R.J., was it? R.J. looked a little like an old photograph he'd once seen of his father when the senior Maitland was younger. And Anna had his eyes, although Rafe'd never seen that degree of kindness in his father's eyes. Mostly there had been scorn or anger.

Because everyone was staring at him, he grappled with his discomfort at the revelation. He looked at Megan. "Any more brothers and sisters hiding somewhere I should know about?"

She offered him a sympathetic smile, immediately putting herself in his position and empathizing. "None that I know of."

Which wasn't altogether reassuring, given his father's penchant for showgirls and seduction, Rafe thought. But he nodded, taking his aunt at her word. Instinct told him she wouldn't lie to him. Which made him feel a little guilty, but that was another story. He had enough to deal with right now.

"Hell of a surprise, isn't it?" R.J. asked, putting out his hand toward his newly discovered sibling. "It is for me, too. Most baby brothers arrive in diapers, not boots." He nodded at the worn cowboy boots Rafe was wearing to underscore his point.

In the midst of the emotional turmoil, Greer realized she'd forgotten to get Rafe a pair of appropriate shoes. Another oversight. She wasn't usually this disorganized, not when it came to details that were related to her job. She had to get centered, she ordered herself silently. But ever since she'd seen Rafe walking toward her, she seemed to have misplaced her efficient manner as well as several other things.

"I'm Anna," the woman said to Rafe in case he hadn't gotten her name. She playfully elbowed her older brother out of the way. "Welcome to the family." She bypassed the hand he'd put out and threw her arms around him in a warm, welcoming embrace. "There's always room for one more."

Still somewhat numbed, he figured that was a matter of opinion. As far as he was concerned, it was already far too crowded.

Resigned, Rafe remained where he was as both R.J. and Anna ushered forward their respective spouses. After that, Megan commandeered him again and followed up with introductions to his cousins and cousins-in-law. He supposed that he should be grateful that Megan had decided that for the time being, his cousins' children wouldn't be present.

Not that he was about to remember any of the names or faces that swam by him, he thought, feeling overwhelmed and definitely outnumbered.

"And that's all of us," Megan finally declared, giving Rafe's arm an affectionate, reassuring squeeze.

"Don't worry." A willowy brunette he recalled as being introduced to him as Megan's daughter, Abby, came up to his other side. "There won't be a quiz for at least a week."

The same tall, thin butler who had admitted them came into the room to announce that dinner was being served. His ordeal, Rafe thought with resignation, was only just beginning.

"Shall we?" Megan asked, once more hooking her arm through Rafe's. Without waiting for his agreement, she began leading him to the dining room.

"He looks a little overwhelmed," Abby commented to Greer, her voice low. Hugh surprised her by coming up to her other side and taking her arm. Together, they all left the living room for the dining area. "I would be, too, if I was meeting this crowd for the first time," Abby was saying. "We never gave Rafe a chance to say more than three words." She looked at Bethany. "Is this his baby?"

Greer had almost forgotten she was still holding the toddler. Bethany had dozed through most of the excitement.

"No, this is his—" What did she call Bethany until things were ironed out and became official? Greer hadn't a clue. She turned to an archaic word that didn't begin to reflect the depth of feeling she knew was involved. "His ward, Bethany."

"Ward?" Hugh's interest was aroused as he looked down at the baby.

Abby smiled, lightly running her hand over the downy head. "You're too little to be something that cold, aren't you, Beth?" She raised her eyes to Greer's face. "She's beautiful."

For reasons she couldn't begin to fathom, Greer felt pride flicker through her at the compliment. It didn't begin to make any sense to her, since she had no real ties to either Bethany or Rafe, but it was there, anyway, bright and warm.

"You think all babies are beautiful," Jake teased, coming up behind them. He placed a friendly hand on his older sister's shoulder.

Abby sniffed. "Well, they are." She looked at Greer for support. "Aren't they?"

Mrs. Malone had told anyone who would listen that she'd been the plainest baby ever to arrive at the orphanage. The woman's voice still rang in her head sometimes. *Plain she was born and plain she will die.* It was a terrible legacy to carry around, Greer thought. She'd never managed to get out from under it.

"I wouldn't know. I haven't seen all the babies in the world."

Jake laughed, tickled. "Good answer."

In the dining room, Megan relinquished her hold on Rafe, waving him to a seat. Crossing to Greer now, she swatted her ex-CIA operative son back.

"Don't start flirting with her, Jake. You're a married man now. And besides, she's spoken for." Megan exchanged looks with Hugh before tapping on the side of a glass with her fork to get everyone's attention, no easy feat, given the level of the din in the room. "Everyone, I have an announcement." Eyes turned her way as conversations dissolved or were placed temporarily on hold. "I got so excited introducing Rafe to everyone and everyone to Rafe I forgot to tell you all that in the true spirit of the Marrying Maitlands, Rafe and Greer have become engaged.''

The others, seated at the long dining table, exchanged incredulous looks.

She knew what they were thinking, Greer thought. That they couldn't see someone who looked like Rafe tying himself for life to someone as plain as she was. Though the engagement was entirely a ruse, the reaction she perceived still bothered her. She supposed that made her shallow, but she couldn't seem to block it out.

Abby got over her surprise first. "Well, I think it's wonderful." Taking her wineglass, she raised it high. "Here's to love, wherever and how it may find you." She looked at her husband beside her before continuing. Her smile was sincere as it took in both Greer and Rafe. "I hope you're both very happy together."

Taking her place at the table beside Rafe, Greer mimicked the gesture and lifted up her glass in a toast. This was getting out of hand, she thought. Now it was a battalion of Maitlands she was lying to. Where was this going to end?

"So I guess this is love at first sight at work?" Connor, Megan's oldest son, asked.

Guilt flushed over her. Greer looked to see if

Connor was smirking, but to her surprise he seemed sincere in his question.

"No," Megan corrected him, "actually Greer informs me that this is the second time around for them." Her warm smile widened. "They had a summer romance some years ago."

"Really?" Anna asked, leaning forward, her eyes bright. "Where, when?"

"You'll have to forgive Anna," R.J. teased. "Her eyes light up at the slightest hint of romance."

"Like I'm the only one." Anna looked at her older brother pointedly before shifting her gaze to include his wife.

R.J. inclined his head and laughed, retreating. "Point taken."

"Cease and desist, you two. This isn't about you," Abby told them, then looked at Greer. "So tell us," she urged.

On the spot, Greer had no choice but to repeat the story she'd told Megan earlier, adding a layer here, a layer there, trying desperately to remember what she'd read that one time she'd taken Rachel's diary and hidden with it in her room. She'd learned to live vicariously, beginning to resign herself even at that young age to the fact that love was something that was never going to find her.

As she told her tale, Greer kept her fingers

crossed that no one knew her age. There was a five-year discrepancy between her and Rafe, and though it might not mean that much now, it would have meant a great deal back then.

Throughout her brief recitation, she noticed that Rafe remained silent. She couldn't help wondering what, if anything, was going on in his mind about these lies that were multiplying faster now than rabbits. The initial lie was his, but she was adding to it, giving it breadth and life, and she couldn't help feeling immensely deceitful, even though she was doing it for all the right reasons.

"Where are you two going to settle down after the wedding?" Jake asked when she finished filling them in.

"Does this mean Mother's going to have to break in a brand-new assistant?" R.J. asked before she had a chance to answer.

Not that she could answer. This was a detail that hadn't occurred to her. She looked at Rafe. They needed to talk. Extensively, before more questions they were unprepared for came their way.

Noting that she'd suddenly been rendered speechless, Rafe came to Greer's rescue. She was coming through far better than he'd imagined and he owed it to her to get her off the hook.

"We haven't worked everything out yet," Rafe told them, wiping the fine layer of applesauce from all of Bethany's fingers with a cloth napkin as he talked. Megan had had a high chair brought in and placed at the table at his side. The woman apparently thought of everything. "Right now, we're just taking this one day at a time."

Megan nodded her approval. "Very sensible." She put down her fork, turning to her nephew. "And when the time comes, you can have the wedding here." She looked at Anna across the table. "I'm sure Anna would love to take care of the details."

By her wide smile, Greer could tell that Anna would like nothing better. "You're talking my language."

She'd forgotten that Anna was a wedding planner. Her mind a blank, Greer forced a grateful smile to her lips. She didn't dare look at Rafe right now, afraid that her distress might come to the surface for the others to notice.

"You really don't have to put yourselves out this way, Mrs. Maitland."

"Nonsense, you're family—or will be once the vows are taken. And the Maitlands love to do things in a big way, don't we—people?"

Jake caught the near slip as he knew the others did. "You were going to say 'children,' weren't you, Mother?" he chided teasingly.

Trapped, Megan saw no reason to deny it. "Well,

you are, you know. You are my children.'' Her gaze took in the entire table except for the man at her left. "All of you, and I wouldn't have it any other way."

Megan looked at Rafe. He hadn't said very much during this entire exchange and she thought she knew the reason why. Though only a distant relation to Connor by virtue of the fact that Clyde, Connor's natural father, was a distant relation to the Maitlands, Rafe and Connor were very much alike. Connor played his emotions very close to the chest and, so it seemed, did Rafe.

"I'm sorry, we've embarrassed you,'' she guessed. "You'll have to forgive us, Rafe, we take some getting used to." Her hand over his, she patted it, thinking how, months earlier, she'd assured Connor in just this fashion when he'd finally made his identity known to the others after having been lost to the family for nearly forty years. "But we're a very affectionate, emotional group and we do mean well.''

R.J. laughed, taking a sip of his wine before saying, "Which is Mother's way of saying, put up with it if we butt in. Maybe the man wants a small wedding or to get married in the middle of the desert, under the stars with only the cacti as witnesses. Give him a little room before you start making plans, Mother.''

Instead of arguing the point or taking umbrage at her son's gentle reproach, Megan inclined her head toward Rafe. "He's right, I should back off." As was typical of her, Megan took on the entire blame for the situation getting out of hand. "But we do mean well," she repeated.

Something told Rafe that she was not merely feeding him rhetoric, but meant that from the bottom of her heart. Again, he found himself liking the woman. Just the way Greer had promised that he would.

"I bet you're glad that's all over with," Greer commented as they began to walk toward the guesthouse together. It was probably the longest three and a half hours he'd ever spent, she guessed, although she'd had trouble reading his expression during the course of the evening. He was certainly playing the part of the long lost nephew who was glad to be back in the bosom of his family well. If she hadn't known any better, she would have said that he actually meant it.

Rafe laughed quietly to himself at her observation. The baby was tucked against his chest. Bethany had fallen asleep shortly after dinner and had spent the next hour and a half nestled against Megan, who had taken her into her arms right after dessert. If he tried, he could still detect some of his aunt's scent on the baby. He realized that, for some reason, the light fragrance gave him a sense of peace.

"I've been more comfortable," he admitted with a half shrug, watching the baby to make sure that he didn't accidentally wake her. "Though I guess they're not so bad."

She thought that was rather a paltry judgment for the Maitlands. "By and large, they're the finest bunch of people I've ever met."

He slowed his already slow pace. The night was warm and the stars were out, and for once he was in no hurry to be alone again just yet. "You're pretty sold on them, aren't you?"

She shrugged, knowing that in his eyes she probably seemed pandering or subservient. But it wasn't like that. She truly liked the family she'd observed from the sidelines these last few months at the clinic as Megan's chief assistant. She liked the way they were all independent but immediately banded together whenever there was any sign of trouble. She would have given anything to have been part of that. Even by proxy.

Greer smiled to herself, thinking of her situation. Maybe, in a way, she was. Until, of course, the engagement ruse was over.

But for now, she could pretend...

"Very," she answered. She glanced back toward

the house and saw that Megan was standing on the patio that overlooked the rear of the property, with Hugh beside her. They made a nice couple, she thought. Megan waved at them. Greer waved back. "I guess Mrs. Maitland wants to see you safely home."

She indicated the main house and Megan when Rafe looked at her quizzically.

His own parents had let him do what he wanted when he wanted at a very young age. At first he'd thought of it as freedom, then later recognized it for what it was: apathy on his father's part. His mother had cared, but she'd been so wrapped up in her own problems that she had viewed his absence as something to be grateful for. He was one less problem she had to deal with. It felt odd to have someone care what he was doing now that he was twenty-five.

He nodded toward the house. "She's going to expect us to kiss good night."

Butterflies piloted huge jets in her stomach. Greer could feel each one of the hairs on her head as she turned back to face him.

"Then I guess we had better give her what she expects." Had that come from her? She hardly felt her lips moving.

A smile curved his mouth as Rafe looked at her. "I guess."

Shifting the sleeping baby to his other side, Rafe cupped the back of Greer's head with his hand and brought her to him. Their eyes met a second before he lowered his mouth to hers and kissed her.

And ripped open the sky.

Chapter 7

Greer caught her breath.

And then had it snatched away from her again.

Every butterfly-piloted jet flying in her stomach instantly crashed and went up in flames. The longing that she felt spring up within her had its roots in something that had been created in fantasy when she'd been a lonely child. It had been held in abeyance all these years. Waiting for the right daydream, the right man.

Waiting for him.

Knowing it was wrong, powerless to stop it, Greer could feel herself melting in the heat of Rafe's kiss as it unfurled and spread out to every single space within her body. Claiming it.

Claiming her.

Without meaning to, without being fully aware of what she was doing, she slipped her hands around his neck and leaned into the kiss. Leaned into his iron-hard, sizzling body. Determined to absorb every moment, every single sensation.

He'd made no conscious decision to do it, yet Rafe found himself deepening the kiss. And liking it. Liking the rush that overwhelmed him as the seconds ticked by, slipping into eternity. His hand slipped from cupping her head to caressing her back, pressing her to him.

He'd seen lightning striking a tree once, bringing it down within moments. But lightning always gave some kind of a warning and rarely came flashing out of nowhere. There'd been no warning here. Not really. A vague suggestion perhaps when he'd accidentally brushed his lips over Greer's earlier in the day.

But not this. Certainly not this.

He felt himself felled as surely as that tree that the lightning bolt had brought down in his boss's front yard during a storm two years ago.

Not entirely certain just what was going on with him, Rafe finally stepped back, more than a little dazed. He looked at Greer, really looked at her for the first time, though it wasn't as easy as it sounded. It felt as if his eyes saw everything in a haze.

Her face was soft, delicate. Because of the glasses she wore, he hadn't realized that she had high cheekbones. On closer scrutiny, he could see them. It gave her a slightly sexy, vulnerable look. Intrigued, stirred, he wondered if she could be convinced to switch to contact lenses. He had a feeling she was almost hiding behind those glasses.

All in all, she did herself a huge disservice by retreating into an image of someone far older than she actually was. As he studied Greer's face, he saw the untried young girl who still remained inside. The one he'd tasted on his lips. And it made Rafe wonder. A great deal.

He glanced toward the front door just beyond them. Desire nudged forward, reminding him just how long it had been since he'd been with a female who didn't need her diaper changed periodically.

"Would you like to come in?"

Rafe's voice was coming at her from a great distance, and it took her a moment to understand what he was saying to her.

"Yes. *No.*" The second word came quickly, emphatically on the heels of the first as she realized what she'd just said and the implications of that reply. Greer felt herself growing even more flustered than she already was. Greer swallowed, wishing she was more articulate. "I mean, it's been a very long day for both of us and I should be getting back. I..."

Her cheeks were turning pink again. Rafe touched her hair, amused by her reaction. Curious. The women he knew were light-years away from this one. He didn't think half a blush could be mustered between all of them.

"What are you afraid of?"

The question whispered along her skin. Everything, she thought, wishing it was otherwise. Wishing she was stronger than she was. Vainly she squared her shoulders, trying to appear unfazed.

"Nothing. I'm not afraid." Her answer was hurried, breathless, as if she were trying to outrun something she didn't know how to handle. "It's just that I have a full day tomorrow and there are the others to try to locate and the party to plan and there's a fund-raiser at the end of the month..." She ran out of steam.

His eyes told her he saw through her. That he knew exactly what she was thinking, exactly what she was feeling. His smile was warm, gentle, rather than condescending, and she took heart in it.

"It's all right," he said softly. "I'll see you tomorrow. Good night."

He was already slipping through the doorway with Bethany.

"Good night," she murmured to the closed door before finally turning away.

It's all right.

His words, his voice echoed in her head.

No, she thought as she made her way back to the car that she'd left in front of the main house, it wasn't all right. She was behaving like some frightened little rabbit in a pet shop, fearful of every hand that reached out to pet her. She certainly wasn't behaving like the consummate businesswoman she had, with great pains, managed to turn herself into.

Angry with herself, Greer yanked open the door on the driver's side. All right, so the man was drop-dead gorgeous, so what? He was her boss's nephew and five years younger than she was to boot. Greer dropped into her seat and tugged on the seat belt. Was she so desperate that she was thinking about robbing the cradle for a few stolen moments of excitement? Of pleasure? The kind of pleasure she'd never had the chance to experience?

She wasn't robbing anything, she declared silently, slamming the door. If anything, the cradle was robbing her. Robbing her of her poise, of her assurance. Of everything she'd worked so hard these last eight years to achieve…

All she had was the facade she'd crafted so carefully, and she'd thank him to take his lips back and leave her that.

With an uncustomary sharp turn of the wheel, Greer peeled out of the driveway—also uncustomary for the careful driver she always tried to be.

She didn't sleep much that night. And when she did manage to drop off, her dreams were all of him. Of a heated mouth that melted all her bones and fricasseed her brain until she was reduced to nothing more than pulsating needs and desires.

By the time she woke up with a jolt the second time, she decided that maybe it was safer just to remain awake for the rest of the night.

The darkness in her room wrapped itself around her like a stifling cloak, reminding her just how alone she really was.

Greer allowed the myriad details that were part of her job to engulf her for the next few days. All told, the work took her mind off her private life. Especially her feelings. If she didn't think about them, didn't think about the way Megan Maitland's tall, dark and sexy nephew undid her composure, everything she'd experienced when he'd kissed her in front of the guesthouse would eventually fade away.

And she wanted it to fade away. In the worst way. Because there was absolutely no reason for the memory, the sensation, to exist other than to tantalize her, to tease her and make her yearn for the impossible. There was obviously no future in any of this. The man would be gone out of her life as soon as the charade and the reunion were tucked safely away in the past.

And if she allowed herself to daydream, allowed herself to think that there was more than a snowball's chance in hell that perhaps he'd have some kind of feelings for her, the disappointment that she knew would be waiting for her might be too much for her to handle.

Fear of the yawning, steely jaws of disappointment had kept her from letting her heart be tempted before, at least by a man. It was enough that she'd allowed the dream of a family to raise her hopes over and over again when she was younger. Look where that had gotten her. Nowhere. She'd had her hopes dashed again and again, only to ultimately find herself still alone, still without a family to call her own.

She didn't want to go through that kind of roller-coaster ride on the romantic front. Something told her that at her age, the result would be that much more devastating.

It was best not to begin something that would never have a happy ending.

Greer smiled to herself, typing a memo on her computer as she sat within the spacious office that came with being Megan Maitland's right hand. Romantic front, right. She and romance didn't even have so much as a nodding acquaintance, and it was best for everyone if it remained that way. There was no point in giving in to any wild flights of fantasy.

Despite all her logical arguments to the contrary, the taste of his lips insisted on remaining with her.

A sigh escaped. He'd kissed her.

Of course he'd kissed her, Greer mocked herself. His aunt was standing there, watching, and he was pretending to be her fiancé. He couldn't very well have kicked her in the shins, now could he?

And if the kiss had gotten a little more intense than she'd anticipated, there was an explanation for that, too. Several explanations, actually. One was that she had no idea what it felt like to be kissed by a man. She'd shied away from every would-be encounter. Maybe men kissed like that when it meant nothing, how was she to know the difference?

The other explanation was that Rafe was just taking advantage of the moment. She'd heard that men did that and, in her own defense, kissing her had to be better than kissing a post, she thought.

Didn't it?

"D'you know that your brow furrows when you concentrate?"

Her fingers slipped on the keyboard and words

appeared on the computer screen that couldn't be found in any dictionary in the known universe.

Startled, Greer looked up to see that Rafe was standing in her doorway, his arms folded in front of his chest. A chest that looked wider than it had the last time she'd seen him.

Or was that just her imagination?

How long had he been standing there like that? From the way Rafe was leaning against the doorjamb, he appeared to have been watching her for at least a couple of minutes, if not longer.

Embarrassed, she tried to speak. Her throat felt as if she'd just swallowed an entire peanut butter sandwich without the benefit of any liquid lubricant. Words stuck to the roof of her mouth.

"What?" she finally squeaked out miraculously.

Rafe crossed to her, mildly entertained by the way she was transformed from a woman lost in deep thought to one who appeared completely flustered. It was like night and day. Did he do that to her, or was she like that with every man? Though he knew exactly what he looked like, he'd never flattered himself that he had any undue effect on a woman.

"When you concentrate, your brow furrows." Rafe nodded toward the computer monitor. "What are you working on?"

As he came around to stand behind her and look

at the screen, she turned off the monitor, feeling extremely foolish at being caught this way. She lifted a shoulder in a dismissive half shrug.

"Just some reports."

"Top secret?" he asked innocently, hooking his thumbs in the loops of his jeans.

Because her brain was suddenly doing an imitation of laundry in the spin cycle, she was having trouble following him. "Excuse me?"

Rafe gestured toward the screen. "Well, you turned the monitor off. I was just wondering if those reports you're working on are supposed to be on some kind of a need-to-know basis." Though why that would apply to a nonprofit clinic was beyond him.

She'd turned the monitor off because she'd been lost in thought about him and there *was* nothing on her screen to have captured her attention so completely. Nothing but the gibberish she'd just accidentally typed when he'd startled her. If he saw that, he'd continue questioning her and she had no answers to give him that wouldn't make her look foolish.

"No, I just don't like people looking over my shoulder."

She was aware that Rafe was now touching that same shoulder, resting his fingers easily on her silk blouse. She could feel the heat penetrating from his hand, slipping through the material and seeping into her skin. You'd think the material would have acted as some sort of insulator, instead of feeling as if it was being entirely burned away just by the passing of his hand.

Greer took a deep breath, hoping she sounded nonchalant. ''So what are you doing here?''

Because she was addressing the question to her now-darkened monitor, Rafe turned her swivel chair around until she was facing him. With his hands on the armrests on either side of her, he leaned into her slightly before answering.

''Looking for you.''

Greer could feel her heart vibrating as it made an unexpected trip to her throat and lodged itself there. Perhaps forever. She fervently hoped that it wasn't apparent to him.

''Oh?'' Her voice sounded reedy to her own ear. ''Why?''

A hint of amusement crept into his magnetic eyes. ''Because people who are supposed to be wildly in love usually tend to want to see each other more than once every few days.''

''Wildly in love?'' she repeated, feeling her kneecaps seceding from the rest of her.

Could one walk with no kneecaps? she wondered desperately. If she stood up now, would she just wind up collapsing bonelessly back into her chair and embarrass herself?

She was afraid to test out the theory. Besides, he wasn't backing away, and he blocked her avenue of escape even if she could get her legs to work.

Rafe nodded in response. "Wildly in love," he repeated. "Otherwise, why would we have gotten engaged so quickly?"

She had no answer for that, nor for anything else he might think to ask right now. Her mind had turned into a complete blank. All she could think of was how it felt to have him standing so close to her. So close that if she made more than the slightest movement, parts of her body would be brushing suggestively against parts of his.

Her breath was going the way of her kneecaps, making a speedy exit. Greer tried to pull it back.

"Um, why else indeed," she muttered, stalling for time and searching for a grain of composure.

Damn it, why was he doing this to her? Why was he unraveling her as if she was a dropped spool of thread that was rolling haphazardly down an incline? Did it amuse him, give him some sort of superior pleasure?

Maybe she could divert him, send him off until she got her bearings. Anything was worth a try. She said the first thing that came to her. "Have you seen your aunt?"

He knew what she was trying to do and managed to keep the smile from his lips. He was beginning to think that "flustered" looked kind of cute on her. "She's the one who told me where to find you."

After expressing her pleasure at seeing him, Megan had taken Rafe to the day-care center where she'd had him leave Bethany. She said it was so that the little girl could get the benefit of being around other children her age. He'd been forced to agree. It had also freed him to visit as long as he liked without worrying about Bethany.

As they talked briefly before she left for her meeting, Megan had offered to introduce him to a number of ranchers in the area with the suggestion that perhaps he'd find something here to his liking.

"I'll be glad to stake you or arrange for a loan if something catches your interest," she'd told him. There'd been no mention of collateral, no coy wordplay about interest as he might have expected. Only a sincere offer of help.

Even now, after he'd left Megan at the day-care center, Rafe was still trying to figure out if the woman was on the level, or just exceedingly clever.

But if she was being clever, to what end? It shouldn't have made any difference to her whether he remained in Austin or returned to Nevada.

In any event, instead of a ranch, the only thing that had caught his interest in Austin so far was the woman he was bracketing with his arms right now. Rafe was accustomed to judging horseflesh, and he judged it both quickly, and then slowly, to evaluate the hidden assets. He decided that it was only fair to apply the same rule of thumb to Greer.

The more he looked at her, the more he saw.

The features that had initially struck him as plain weren't quite plain, he realized now. There were facets there, layers. And she had beautiful eyes that intrigued him.

Not to mention that he had a sneaking suspicion that beneath those loose clothes she favored so much was a figure that could stand some looking into.

His thoughts surprised him, just as they had done the other night. Thinking about women, especially wondering about them, didn't usually enter into his day-to-day dealings. Women were something on the periphery of his world, like newspapers and airplanes. He was aware of them, but he didn't ordinarily avail himself of anything they had to offer.

Somehow, Greer was different. The puzzle was how.

He'd think about that later, when he was alone, he decided. For now, he'd settle on filling a stomach that was about to run on empty. Though Megan had invited him to go into the kitchen in the main house any time he wished and either help himself or ask the cook to prepare something for him, he'd settled on relying on himself. He didn't care for being waited on. Breakfast had been scrambled eggs, burned around the edges because he still hadn't gotten the hang of the stove, and toast, burned because he liked it that way.

Still, breakfast had been hours ago and he was hungry. Very hungry, he thought, looking at her intently.

Rafe straightened up. "How about joining me for some lunch?"

Not about to let the answer to his question turn out to be negative, Rafe was already taking her hand and coaxing her from her seat.

Mercifully, he'd finally backed away and left her breathing space. But not before he'd filled every inch of that space with the cologne he wore. Something tantalizing that turned every bone in her body to mush.

It was a condition she was becoming familiar with with a fair amount of regularity.

Greer struggled to pull her dissolving thoughts together. "Is it lunchtime already?"

Wonderful repartee, Greer. He's going to think he's in the presence of the clinic's resident wit.

"Already and past," he assured her, indicating his watch. Looking down at it, Greer saw that it was just a little after one. "C'mon," he was saying, "if we're going to get anyone to believe we're engaged, we have to spend a little time together."

To her surprise, her knees were still in working order as he drew her to her feet.

Still, in a last-ditch effort to save herself, she nodded at the dormant computer screen. "I do have a lot of work..."

He wasn't about to let her talk her way out of it. Especially since he could feel that her resistance would cave in quickly if a little pressure was applied. His aunt had commented on how nice they seemed together and he was all for promoting that. A lot was riding on promoting that image.

Besides, he did like the idea of sharing Greer's company for the space of a meal. In an odd way, he found her appealing. That didn't happen very often.

"People work better when they take a break or two during the day," he told her. "It refreshes their thinking."

She was surprised at his philosophy. Or that he even had a philosophy at all. Maybe he wasn't just a pretty cowboy, all looks and muscle and very little brain.

The thought made her hesitate. She knew she was ultimately much safer behind her desk. The last thing she needed was to add more fuel to these feelings that threatened to storm over her like revolutionaries storming the Bastille.

Still, she had made a bargain with him and to refuse now would be going back on her word, something she refused to do. "Maybe you're right."

"I usually am," he told her, winding his fingers more tightly around hers. He looked around. "You have a purse or something you need to take with you?"

Her purse was more of a business tool than something she felt she needed with her when she went out socially. But it did have her wallet in it. Was she assuming too much?

She caught her lower lip between her teeth. "Not if you're buying."

Rafe looked at her as if she'd just impugned his integrity. "I'm the man."

His answer made her smile. Greer began to relax a little. "That doesn't automatically mean anything anymore."

His gaze swept over her from head to foot, as if he were taking full measure of her. She could almost feel it as it passed over her. Again, her breath insisted on lodging itself in her throat. The condition was threatening to become a permanent one.

"It does to me."

She'd come to consider that way of thinking as

Neanderthal. Why did hearing him espouse it fill her with a sense of sweetness now?

What was wrong with her? Why couldn't she think straight? Why was he scrambling all of her circuits so badly? He was just a man. A being comprised of tissues and bones and blood vessels...

Yes, but those tissues and bones and blood vessels all seemed to be so beautifully arranged, a small voice within her whispered.

Somehow, she managed to find her tongue. "I take it you're the old-fashioned type."

Although that wasn't strictly true, she realized. An old-fashioned male wouldn't diaper a baby or concern himself with all the details involved with making a baby comfortable the way he did. And an old-fashioned male wouldn't be trying to secure single-parent custody.

His frown dismissed the label. "Old-fashioned, new-fashioned, only one fashion as far as I'm concerned. The right fashion." Still holding her hand, something she was acutely aware of, he drew her toward the doorway. "Now, let's go."

For the first time since she'd met him, genuine amusement began to edge its way forward for Greer. "Whatever you say, 'fiancé.'"

His eyes met hers. She could almost feel his smile as it slowly slipped along his lips, curving them. "As long as we're clear about that."

She found herself staring at the back of his head, fighting the urge to run her fingers through his hair, as he led the way.

But their exit was blocked by the tall, rangy man who suddenly materialized out of nowhere and stood in the doorway. Surprised, Greer took a step back. Though she didn't know everyone who worked at the clinic by name, part of her job was to coordinate all the different departments, so she knew most of them by sight.

She didn't know this man.

The look the stranger gave her was polite, curious. As an afterthought, he nodded at Rafe, but his words were addressed to Greer. "Excuse me, are you Greer Lawford?"

Out of the corner of his eye, Rafe saw Greer transformed again. Gone was the uncertain young woman, to be replaced by someone who was all business.

"Yes?"

The stranger entered the room without waiting for an invitation. "They told me to come to see you about the job. My name's Mick Hanon."

Chapter 8

Greer shook her head at the man who was standing just inside the room.

"I'm afraid someone misinformed you, Mr. Hanon," she told him. "I don't handle the hiring for the clinic. You need to see—"

He cut her off. "Not *a* job, *the* job." The dark-haired man laughed easily. "Sorry, I guess I'm not making myself clear. I'm already hired. I'm working at the construction site," he added, in case that wasn't obvious from the jeans and work shirt he had on or the hard hat he was holding in his hand. "But the foreman said I was just supposed to check in with you before I got started." He jerked a thumb toward the western end of the building, beyond which the new wing was going up. "Something about a form to sign?"

Rafe's sudden appearance on what she considered to be her territory had really disoriented her, Greer thought with disgust. There was no other explanation for forgetting the fact that Mrs. Maitland had her keeping a running file on all the people brought in to work on the new west wing. It had to do with the paperwork required by worker's compensation in case any of them were injured while on the job.

Greer's mouth curved in an apologetic smile. "I'm sorry, you're right. I'm afraid things are a little hectic around here right now." Reaching over to her desk, she extracted a folder that had doubled in size since the first of the month. She flipped it open and pulled out a fresh form. "What did you say your name was again?"

"Mick Hanon. Two *n*'s separated by an *o*." As he spelled it for her, he made no attempt to hide the fact that he was looking Rafe over and taking the measure of him the way one man did of another when on uncertain ground. Mick Hanon had his own reasons for taking this job and lack of funds was not among them.

"Now, if you'll just sign this." Greer turned the

single page around on her desk to face him and offered Mick a pen.

Taking it, he scanned the page quickly, then wrote his signature in the appropriate place.

She turned the page back around, jotted a couple of notes down beneath Mick's name, then closed the folder. She made a mental note to transcribe everything onto the computer when she returned as a backup.

Finished, she glanced up at Mick. "There, painless."

Mick nodded politely. Hopefully, that was a prophesy, he thought.

Donning his hard hat, he began to back out of the office. "Okay, then, I'd better get back to work. Maybe we'll see each other again," he added as he tipped his hat to her.

Greer suddenly became aware that Rafe had slipped his hand to her shoulder in a manner that could only be called proprietary. As if he was staking his claim lest the other man get any ideas.

He was playing this charade to the hilt, she thought, trying to squelch the sliver of a thrill she felt when he touched her.

This was a game, nothing more. Getting carried away would only be dangerous.

The silent warning fell several feet short of its mark.

"You ready now?" There was just a shade of impatience in Rafe's voice as he asked the question.

There was something else she wanted to note down, she realized, but it would keep. It was certainly not important enough to make Rafe wait any longer. Especially when he seemed to be impatient to get going.

"Yes." She stepped out into the corridor and closed the door behind them. The lock clicked into place. "By the way, where's the light of your life? Bethany," she explained when Rafe didn't respond right away.

He was still trying to figure out why he'd felt so territorial when Hanon had looked at Greer. There certainly hadn't been anything insulting about the man's manner. What the hell was wrong with him? Annoyed with himself, Rafe shook off the mood.

"At the day-care center." He thought it rather poetic to have one on the premises, seeing as how the clinic was mainly concerned with pregnant women. "Megan thought it might be a good idea to have Bethany around other kids near her own age."

Greer noticed that he'd referred to his aunt by only her first name. It was probably going to take him some time to think of the woman as his aunt. How long would it take for Rafe to adjust to the idea that he had a half brother and sister he'd never known anything about?

Maybe it was her imagination, but he didn't seem as resentful or cynical when he mentioned family members as he had been at first. Maybe things were slowly working themselves out.

She found herself being glad for him.

Though he valued his privacy, the silence that accompanied them as they walked out of the building was a shade too quiet for Rafe. He found himself hunting around for a topic.

"So you're a big wheel around here," he finally commented as he led the way to the car Greer had arranged for him to rent. When he'd pulled into the lot earlier, a car in the very first row was just leaving, so the walk was short.

"No, I'm the assistant to the big wheel," Greer corrected him. Attention made her as uncomfortable as flattery did. She worked best behind the scenes, in someone else's shadow, free in her anonymity to do what was necessary. "I'm just there to make sure it's properly greased and running."

There was nothing conceited about her, Rafe thought. A lot of people with far less important positions strutted around as if the world wouldn't rotate on its axis without their help. He had the feeling that had never been the case with Greer. He'd never given humbleness any thought one way or another, but on Greer he had to admit it looked good. He'd never had any patience with the pompous asses of the world.

Rounding the hood, he flipped the car's locks and got in. "Looks like more than that to me."

Greer buckled herself in and shrugged. "There are a great many details that go into running the clinic. I try to make that easier for Mrs. Maitland. Coordinating events, fund-raisers, keeping tabs on insurance issues, things like that."

She made it sound like nothing, but he had a hunch it was one hell of a juggling act. Rafe thought of what had initially brought her into his life.

"What about the Christmas reunion? Seems to me that doesn't have anything to do with running the actual clinic."

It was on the tip of her tongue to ask where they were going, but she let the question go for now. If he'd wanted her to know, he would have told her. Maybe it was a surprise.

The next moment, she laughed at herself for giving the moment qualities that only existed between people when they cared about each other. If she wasn't careful, she really was going to start buying into the illusion they were attempting to create.

Greer redirected her thoughts to the conversation.

"Sure it does. It keeps the head of the clinic and the board happy."

She'd lost him. "The board?"

"Of the clinic," she clarified. "Most of it's comprised of the family—R.J., Anna, Abby—" Greer stopped before she wound up naming all the members of the family. "And the others."

He spared her a glance before turning the steering wheel to the right. He'd studied a map before he'd gone to seek her out, something he knew the others at the ranch back home would have laughed at him for. But he didn't want to look like some hick visiting the "big city" for the first time.

"Any nonfamily members on the board?"

"A few." She knew the names would mean nothing to him if she repeated them. "New blood to keep Maitland Maternity at the apex of medicine as it applies to pregnancies, infertilities and babies."

The clinic was strictly a nonprofit organization, but that didn't mean it had to fall behind the new strides being made. Quite the opposite. Maitland Maternity was considered to be on the cutting edge as far as infertility research and treatments were concerned.

They stopped at a light. "And how do you fit into all this?"

She looked at him oddly. He already knew the

answer to that. It had been the first thing out of her mouth when she'd introduced herself to him in Nevada. They'd just talked about it in the office. "I'm Mrs. Maitland's assistant."

Taking his foot off the brake, he shook his head. "No, I mean in this atmosphere of babies, born, unborn and wished for."

She sat up a little straighter. "You mean because I'm not married and don't have my own family?"

She seemed so cloistered to him, so removed from the very idea of children. Hell, she hadn't even known how to hold Bethany when he'd first handed the little girl to her. At first glance, he would have said she seemed like a fish out of water.

"Something like that."

That seemed a slightly narrow-minded judgment from where she sat. Luckily Mrs. Maitland hadn't thought like him or else she would have missed out on what she viewed as the best opportunity of her life.

"I don't have to be a pilot to appreciate a plane ride," she pointed out. "I like the work that's being done here. I've worked in the corporate world, and frankly, the killer instinct is not pleasant to be around."

She watched familiar places pass by. Where was he taking her? Was he lost? She forced herself to bite back the question. She might not know much about men, but she knew they hated being given directions. She supposed that insulted some basic pathfinder instinct they all thought they were created with.

"What I've witnessed since I came to work for Maitland Maternity has restored my faith in the basic goodness of human nature," she told him. "Your aunt will not allow a single pregnant woman to be turned away, whether or not that woman has the means to pay for the services she needs."

Pressing down on the accelerator, Rafe just made it through a light before it turned red. "So you've said."

She flushed. "I guess I probably sound like a cheering section for your aunt, but I assure you, I'm not alone."

She wasn't ashamed of how she felt about her work or about Megan Maitland. It wasn't every day you found something or someone to believe in.

Just like it wasn't every day you fell in love.

Where had that come from? she wondered, surprised by the last thought. She was going to have to exercise better control over the way her mind meandered.

"Your aunt and Maitland Maternity have done an incredible amount of good in the last twenty-five years. I feel lucky to be working for her."

Rafe glanced at her before looking back at the

traffic. She sounded completely sincere. It rather amazed him. "Way I see it, she's lucky to have you."

That thought had never occurred to her. "Me?"

Her surprise amused him. Didn't the woman have any sense of what she was? "Sure. How many people are willing to go out on a limb and do what you did just so that their 'boss' could get what she wanted?"

He meant the false engagement, Greer realized. "If you're referring to the charade, I honestly thought you were just testing me."

He laughed. He hadn't thought of her as being sharp in that way. "I was. You passed."

"I mean I didn't think you were serious."

"I wasn't, at first," he admitted. He smiled in her direction. "I figured it was the fastest way to get rid of you. But you didn't go."

The confession made her smile. A lot of people made that mistake with her. "I might look like a pushover, but I'm not."

The word was demeaning and not one he'd apply to her now that he was getting to know her. The woman was bright, intelligent and efficient. That didn't spell *pushover* in his book.

"I don't think you look like a pushover."

She remembered the look in his eyes when he'd made the proposition.

"Oh, please, one look at me and you thought you could run over me with one of your smallest horses." She sighed, her mind drifting back before she could shut the memories out. "But I learned a long time ago to stand up for myself. If I didn't, there was nobody else to do it." She dismissed the mood that was overtaking her. "That's why I like your aunt so much. She stands up for other people, for people who can't or no longer have the will to stand up for themselves."

"Pretty altruistic," he commented, still not certain if he completely bought into it, though he had to admit that the more he got to know his aunt, the more he liked her. A little like with Greer, he mused.

"She said it was because she didn't want anyone to go through what she once had."

"And what was that?"

She realized that Rafe knew little about the family he'd suddenly discovered and that the right to explain lay with Megan. But she knew the other woman wouldn't mind if she did a little of the clarifying herself. Megan would want Rafe to understand. "She had a baby out of wedlock when she was seventeen. A baby boy her father told her died at birth."

"But he didn't." Given her tone, Rafe figured it was a safe guess.

She hadn't been there for the initial reunion, but she'd heard the story from Megan one afternoon. There'd been tears in the woman's eyes as she spoke.

"You had dinner with him the other night." Rafe raised a curious brow as he looked at her. "Connor. You and your siblings aren't the only ones who've been missing from her life. Connor was taken away by Mrs. Maitland's father and secretly sold to the senior Maitland for his daughter."

That sounded rather melodramatic for this day and age. She was probably exaggerating. "Sold?"

"In effect. Mrs. Maitland's father was given monetary compensation for the boy." According to Mrs. Maitland, she'd discovered that her father had done it because he felt she was too young to raise a child alone. The money had been set aside to help her, not because he'd wanted to make a profit on her mistake. "Connor was adopted and no one was the wiser for almost forty-five years."

He gathered that there had been some sort of a reckoning that had brought all of this to light. "So what happened?"

Since he knew nothing about Connor, he wouldn't know about his sister's duplicity in the matter. She had no idea if he was close to Janelle or not. Greer became deliberately evasive.

"I'm afraid it'll take more than a short luncheon

to explain.'' She was going to need diplomacy and diplomacy took time.

He picked up on the word. ''Why short? You don't punch a clock, do you?'' He didn't think someone in her position would have to account for her time, especially since he had a feeling that she skipped most of her lunches in deference to her work.

''No, I don't punch a clock, but there's always so much to do.'' She'd wasted most of this morning and she could ill afford to do that. ''I'm never finished.''

Rafe grinned. ''That just translates into job security.''

They drove down the next street in silence.

Maybe he was lost and trying to find his way. She glanced at her watch again. ''Maybe I should be driving.''

He leaned forward to read a sign, his voice testy. ''Why?''

''Because I know the streets better. Are you always this touchy?''

''Pretty much,'' he said honestly, ''when I'm not in my element.''

She knew he'd drifted around a little before settling at the ranch where he now worked. She had a feeling he felt at home there. That gave him a great deal in common with some of the Maitland men. "And that element would be horses."

"Right again." He saw a street he'd noted for himself and felt more at ease. They were almost there. "You know where you stand with horses. They respect a firm, kind hand and will go through fire for the right master."

"So will people," she pointed out. "The key in both cases is the way you treat them."

The light was yellow. This time, instead of racing through it, he came to a stop and looked at her instead. He'd heard something in her voice that caught his attention. "What was it like?"

The question came out of nowhere and she wasn't sure where it was going, either. "What was what like?"

"Being an orphan."

She could feel herself stiffening inwardly, the way she always did when she was aware of the difference between herself and most of the people around her. The ones who'd had parents who'd cared, parents who had been there through good times and bad.

"I wasn't one, technically. I was just abandoned, that's all." Her face forward, she recited the words that defined her childhood. "By one parent before I was born and by the other several years after I came into the world. The loneliness is the same, but the definition is different.''

She wasn't answering the question he'd asked her. ''What was it like for you?'' he pressed.

She looked at him then, puzzled. ''Why do you want to know?''

''Because the judge might ask some probing questions and I don't want to be embarrassed. I need to know how you feel about things.''

It was the first response that occurred to him and he knew it was acceptable, even though it wasn't the entire reason behind his question. He wanted an answer because he was curious. Because he found himself wondering about her, about what made her tick. There was a lot more to her than first impressions would have led him to believe.

Since he'd asked, she allowed herself to remember, though for most of her adult years, she'd made an effort to forget. To blot things out because it served no purpose to remember. And because it hurt too much.

''It was like being asleep and waiting for the nightmare to end and the dream to begin.'' She didn't realize she sighed wistfully, but Rafe noticed. ''With every new family that came into my life, I hoped that this was it, that they'd like me enough to keep me. But for one reason or another, I never 'got kept,''' she said cryptically, shrugging. ''At eighteen, I was freed from the system and was on my own."

It had been one of the most frightening years of her life, but wonderfully liberating at the same time. For the very first time, she had complete control over her own welfare.

"I put myself through school and promised myself I would never have to wear anyone's old clothes again."

He had no idea why the comment suddenly had him envisioning her standing wearing nothing but his old work shirt, the sleeves coming down over her delicate hands, the shirttails draped over her thighs. One look at her and the word *sex* was not the first one to come to mind. Or the second, either. That impression came later. Just when, he wasn't certain, but he knew that the kiss he'd shared with her had made him definitely aware of it.

"How about you?"

She'd turned the tables on him. He watched the road, looking at the numbers on the buildings as he passed them. They had to be near the restaurant, the one Megan had recommended to him earlier today. "What do you mean?"

"Well, you've prodded and probed me. But it's going to be a two-way street. The judge might ask me something personal about you and I don't really know all that much about you."

He laughed shortly as he slowed for another light. "I'm surprised. I thought you had my bio down pat before you hunted me down."

She wasn't altogether sure that she liked the way he phrased that. "I didn't 'hunt you down.' It was my job to find you."

"And you do your job well."

She knew what he was up to. "You're evading the question."

Glancing at her, Rafe raised his brow in innocence. "Which is?"

If he thought she'd give up, then he was in for a surprise. She wasn't kidding about not being a pushover. If anything, she was the exact opposite when it came to attaining a goal. And this time, the goal was information about him.

"If we were in front of the judge right now, what is there about you that I should know?"

"That I like my coffee black. That I don't like to be beholden to any man. Or woman." Which directly contradicted his situation, he thought, seeing as how he'd already talked to Megan about the hearing and she'd told him she was willing to do what she could. But then, this was for Bethany's sake, not his own, and sometimes a man had to be man enough to know he needed help. "That I'm fair. A day's work for a day's wage, nothing less. Maybe more," he added, because he'd been known to pitch in when the going got rough. "And that I'm a hell of a lot older than my birth certificate says."

He was being enigmatic again. For a cowboy, Rafe had a tendency toward the mysterious, she thought. "What does that mean?"

"That means when your father likes to tomcat around and your mother's a former Vegas showgirl with tenth-grade schooling and a fondness for sloe gin fizzes, you grow up really fast, even for Vegas." He thought of what Greer had just said about putting herself through college. His formal education hadn't gone that high. "The school I put myself through was the school of hard knocks."

She looked at him, sympathy mixed with empathy stirring within her. "Sounds like neither one of us had it easy. You had parents—"

"—I had two people who came in and out of my life," he corrected her. That wasn't the definition of *parents* by a long shot as far as he was concerned. That wasn't the kind of parent he intended to be to Bethany.

"—but you might as well not have," she concluded, as if he hadn't said anything. Her smile was kind and unselfconscious. "All in all, I'd say you turned out pretty well."

When she smiled like that, she wasn't half bad, he thought. Maybe even rather pretty. "So did you."

The compliment made her feel restless. Greer looked down at her hands.

"You know, maybe the judge'll buy into this at that." A thought occurred to her. "Have you thought of asking Mrs. Maitland to support you in this? She is your aunt and she does have a great deal of influence. This kind of thing is right up her alley."

"The thought's occurred to me," Rafe allowed evasively.

The moment he said it, she realized that he'd probably already spoken to his aunt about it. Not by his tone, but by the look in his eyes.

"Sorry."

He didn't understand. "For what?"

"For insulting you."

He thought over the last few sentences. Had to be some subtle woman thing, he decided. "Did you?"

She felt her tongue growing thicker as she tried to explain. "I mean, telling you what to do when you've obviously already done it."

She was sharp, all right. He liked that in a woman. "You were being helpful. Why is that insulting?"

Greer looked out the window. "Some people don't like to be told what to do, or thought to be unable to act on their own without prompting."

"I'm touchy," he said, referring to what she'd said earlier. "But I'm not thin-skinned." He pulled into the next lot. There was a quaint Swiss-style chalet at the far end. "We're here." She glanced at her watch the way she had already done several times on the way over. "Can I have your watch?"

Greer looked up. "What?"

"Your watch." Rafe put his hand out. "Can I have it?"

Thinking the request unusual, she took off her wristwatch and handed it to him, then watched Rafe pocket it.

"Okay, let's go." He saw the question in her eyes. "This way, you won't keep looking at it. You'll get it back after lunch," he told her. "If you don't ask me what time it is until we're ready to go."

She opened her mouth to protest, then shut it again, knowing it was useless to say anything. In a way she rather liked the way he took charge.

Rounding the hood of the car, Rafe was about to lead the way to the restaurant, but he stopped and opened her door first.

The smile that curved her mouth came from deep within as she got out and took the arm he offered.

Chapter 9

Rafe closed his hand over the envelope he was holding, crumpling it as he shut the door firmly behind the nondescript little man who had just delivered it. It was a summons to appear in family court back in Nevada at the end of the month.

Damn it, part of him had begun to hope that since he hadn't heard from Lil's uncle and aunt for several weeks, they had changed their minds about wanting to take custody of the baby and this was all going to go away.

But it wasn't. The court had followed up. He'd left word where he was going, so he supposed he shouldn't have been surprised that the process server had found him. But he'd hoped...

That was the dreamer in him, Rafe thought in disgust, tossing the envelope with its letter onto the desk. A tendency to dream was the only real legacy he had from his father.

Except his father's dreams had all involved winning big in some casino in Vegas. All he wanted was to gain custody of the child who had gained custody of his heart.

The gurgle of delight at the far end of the room caught his attention. Rafe crossed to the playpen, where Bethany, sitting on her well-padded bottom, was busy entertaining herself with a myriad of colorful plastic blocks. Currently, she was attempting to see if they were edible, or at least collapsible enough so that they could be stuffed into her small mouth. She was doing her best to make it happen.

Rafe crouched down, looking at her through the white netting. It amazed him how someone so tiny could come to mean so much to him so quickly.

Oddly enough, in a way the same thing was beginning to be true of Greer.

Not that he cared deeply about her, of course, he thought, but he was beginning to look forward to seeing her each day. They'd begun to take their meals together, at first out of necessity to perpetrate the charade and now because he liked the idea of seeing her and talking to her. Unlike the other women he'd known, she was devoid of coyness, of artifice. What he saw was what he got, and he was beginning to think that what he got was far more than he'd initially believed it to be.

Reaching over the top of the playpen, he stroked Bethany's small head. Her soft, downy hair tickled the palm of his hand.

"Don't you give this a second's worry, Beth," he told her. Bethany stopped trying to consume the pink block in her chubby hands and stared at him with huge blue eyes, looking as if she understood every word he was saying to her. "Nobody's taking you away from me. You're not going to have to live with those people, I promise. They wouldn't be nearly good enough to you."

Bethany began to jabber at him in response. He put his own interpretation on her reply. She was placing her faith in him, just as her mother had before her. He wasn't about to let either of them down.

As he watched Bethany go back to her blocks, Rafe tried to understand why two people who obviously had little love in their hearts and who had raised Lil so that she was literally starved for affection when she met Rory, would want to take on the responsibility of raising a baby. Lil had once told him that her aunt and uncle had called her a burden so often while she was growing up, she'd thought that was her middle name.

Why were they contesting custody? It didn't make any sense. But sense or not, he was determined that they weren't going to take Bethany from him and turn her into an unhappy little girl. Not while there was breath left within him. If he had to, he'd marry Greer before that happened. He'd do whatever it took to keep his word. And to keep Bethany.

Standing up, he reached into the playpen and scooped Bethany up into his arms. "C'mon, Beth, you and I are going out."

Bethany squealed her approval.

Lost in thought, Greer ran her fingertips absently along the band of her wristwatch. Becoming aware of what she was doing, she smiled. She was reliving Rafe's confiscating the watch from her and then returning it after a long, leisurely lunch.

She sighed. It wasn't often that she took that much time away from her work. Now that she thought of it, she couldn't remember the last time she'd taken more than a few minutes off to buy a salad or sandwich to go. Meals were something to be worked into her schedule, nothing more.

This time, it had been more.

Her smile widened. When Rafe had returned the watch to her, she'd had trouble closing the clasp. After watching her make two attempts, he'd taken over. She could still feel his long, strong fingers brushing against her wrist as he placed the watch on it and then closed the clasp.

She'd had no idea that the inside of a woman's wrist could be so erotic.

She shook her head. Silly for a grown woman to get carried away with something so ordinary, so trivial. But there had been something in his eyes as he'd looked at her, just for an instant...

No, there wasn't, she insisted sternly. What was wrong with her? What was she doing, having fantasies about a man who could be her younger brother, for heaven's sake...if she'd had a younger brother.

Still...he had taken to coming by and inviting her out to lunch. Or just dropping by to say hello. She knew this was all happening to keep up the illusion that they were engaged, and yet...

And yet, she sighed, leaning her cheek against her hand and feeling giddy. If this was being foolish, so be it. She'd enjoy it as long as it lasted.

"My, you look as if you're a million miles away."

Greer jumped, nearly overturning her by now cold cup of coffee. Catching it just in time, she looked up to see Megan in her doorway.

She was embarrassed at being caught daydreaming like this. "Oh, Mrs. Maitland, I'm sorry, I didn't see you standing there..."

Megan crossed to her desk, an understanding smile on her lips. It wasn't all that long ago that she had been this young. And this much in love. The signs were hard to miss.

"I doubt if you would have seen the entire Mormon Tabernacle Choir standing there. Judging by the expression on your face, you were in a place far more exciting than this." Standing beside Greer, Megan looked at the younger woman. "Was it nice there?"

Because Greer knew a positive answer would add credence to the charade, she didn't attempt to make any denials. "Very nice."

In the face of Greer's happiness, Megan toyed with the idea of retreating, then decided against it. This had to be said just once, then put aside.

"From what I've seen in the last week or so, Rafe seems to be a very nice young man. I especially like that he is so devoted to that little girl of his..."

Greer began to point out the error of Megan's statement, then hesitated. "Well, technically—"

Megan was ahead of her. "Yes, I know, Bethany isn't really his." She slipped a comfortable arm around Greer's shoulders. "Not by birth, but there is a definite bond between them. Blood isn't everything, my dear. It's the heart that counts, not what scientists can detect in a laboratory." She knew that to be true firsthand. "You learn that after a while." She looked into Greer's eyes, knowing a little of what the other woman had endured. "I love R.J. and Anna just as much as I do Abby, Jake and the others."

"And Connor?" Greer heard herself asking. Curiosity had gotten the better of her. She flushed. She wasn't usually so intrusive. "I'm sorry, Mrs. Maitland. I shouldn't have—"

But Megan was quick to wave away the apology and concern.

"No, that's all right, I don't mind talking about that." Taking a seat next to the desk, Megan continued, controlled passion in her voice. "Connor is my firstborn and there is normally a special place in a mother's heart for her firstborn." Her smile was sad as she thought of what had been lost and would never be regained.

"He's supposed to be the one you cut your teeth on, the one you practice on." The sigh that escaped was small, resigned. Megan always believed in making the best of everything. "Because of circumstances, both Connor and I were denied that kind of bonding. He was a stranger to me when he came into my life, so we went through another sort of bonding period before I discovered the truth."

There had been something about the young man, even then, that had made her receptive toward him even though he had been reserved. "Again, the heart was the main instrument involved. In a way, that's why I'm here."

Greer did a quick mental review and came up empty. "I don't understand."

"That's because I'm being obscure." Megan placed her hand over Greer's. "I don't ordinarily meddle, Greer, but I am very fond of you."

Greer smiled. If the other woman only knew how much that meant to her. "Please, meddle. I've never had anyone care enough to meddle before."

Megan laughed. "Then prepare to be meddled with. But remember, you asked for this." And then Megan sobered just a little. This concern had been very much on her mind since Greer had told her about the engagement. "Greer, you don't think that perhaps you're going just a little too fast?"

Uneasy, Greer looked down at her hands, wondering if Mrs. Maitland was going to say something to the effect that she'd had a change of heart. That she had decided that Greer wasn't good enough to be part of the family.

Mrs. Maitland wasn't the type, Greer silently argued. She wasn't like that.

"No," Greer replied slowly. "When you've

been stuck on 'hold' all of your life, you welcome something happening quickly for once."

To her relief, Megan smiled again and patted her hand. "All right, then. I just want to make sure you're sure before you take that large step."

Greer's mind had gone completely blank. "Large step?"

"Marriage."

Of course. The woman probably thought she was being an idiot. She let go of the breath she was holding, framing her reply carefully.

"I've thought about it. I can't think of anything more wonderful than being married to Rafe." As she spoke, Greer realized that she didn't have to concentrate to form her answer. Her feelings were pushing the words out. "Sure he's gruff at times and maybe a little abrupt, but he's kind and gentle, and the way he is around Bethany is incredible."

She could feel sunshine filling her as she spoke about Rafe and thought of what married life with him would be like. It was just to make this more believable, she argued silently, nothing more. She thought of what he'd told her about his late friend's aunt and uncle.

"Bethany really has no one to love her and Rafe's so determined to be there for her." Before she could think better of it, Greer added, "I wish there'd been someone like that for me when I was growing up.''

Moved, Megan stroked Greer's hair. She knew what it meant to be motherless.

"I know, dear, I know. And I don't want you to think our little talk here in any way means that I'm not welcoming you into the family with open arms, because I am.'' Her throat was tight with emotion as she continued. "Since Rafe's parents are both gone, that puts me at the head of his branch of the family as well, and on behalf of everyone, I'd like to say that it would be an honor to have you join us.'' Holding back her own tears, Megan saw one slip down Greer's cheek. "Oh, Greer, I didn't mean to make you cry.''

Embarrassed, Greer waved away the other woman's apology. "I just get sentimental at times,'' she demurred, annoyed with herself for not having more self-control.

Especially since none of this was real. She wasn't going to be part of their family, so why was she getting so emotional about it?

Maybe it was because she knew none of this was going to happen and she wanted it to, a small voice within her whispered.

"Is this a bad time?''

Startled, Greer turned to see Rafe standing where Megan had been just a few minutes earlier. Didn't anyone have anything better to do than come here? Upset at being caught like this, she quickly wiped her eyes and pocketed the crumpled tissue.

"No, come in." She rose to her feet, feeling less vulnerable that way. She saw that he was studying her face. "Allergies," she mumbled, hoping he hadn't been standing there long enough to hear anything that had passed between his aunt and her.

Rafe let her have her lie. He'd been standing in the doorway long enough to overhear the exchange between Greer and the woman he was beginning to accept as his aunt. Long enough to feel empathy and sympathy as he'd listened to Greer.

There'd been no abundance of warmth when he'd been growing up, but he had, for a time, connected with his mother and felt that she'd loved him, at least to the best of her limited ability. Not to have anyone, to feel that your mother hadn't wanted you, it had to have been rough going for the woman, he decided. And yet Greer had turned out to be a good person. He supposed the fact still amazed him.

He held up the paper that had brought him here. "The court's officially served me with papers. I've—we've," he amended, looking pointedly at Greer and hoping that Megan hadn't caught the slip, "got to make an appearance at the end of the month."

"Of course." Greer slanted a look toward her

employer. "That is, if it's all right if I take a few days' leave."

With three months until Christmas, there remained a long list of things to tend to. The reunion was still up in the air and there were still Rafe's siblings to find. Neither had answered the invitations that had been sent out. Megan had already asked him about their respective whereabouts.

All he could tell her was that the last time he'd seen them was two years ago, at his parents' funeral. They'd lost contact with one another after that. She knew as much as he did about their location. Probably more.

Megan rose to her feet. "Of course, of course. And if you feel you need the added support, I can join you," she told her nephew. "Otherwise, I'll just draft a letter to the judge on your behalf and send it with Hugh. My lawyer," she added in case Rafe had forgotten. "I insist you use him. He can be very persuasive." Both in the courtroom and out, she added mentally. "Don't worry about the fee. I have him on a family retainer."

Rafe nodded, though he was still uncomfortable about having to be even further in debt to her. Yet he knew there was no other way. He supposed he was still having difficulty adjusting to the fact that someone would put herself out for him for no other reason than that she wanted to. This was a far warmer world than he was accustomed to.

Still, expressing gratitude was difficult for him. ''I would appreciate that.''

''Fine, it's settled, then. I'll go draft that letter.'' She crossed to the doorway. ''It will be nice doing something positive for a change instead of worrying about the next accident.''

Greer was immediately alert. Had she missed something? ''Excuse me?''

Megan saw the expression on her assistant's young face. ''No need to trouble yourself, Greer. You have enough to handle. This really doesn't fall within your jurisdiction, anyway.'' She didn't want Greer becoming concerned. It was enough that she and R.J. were. ''This is more a matter of security. Either that, or a witch doctor,'' she confided in a moment of weariness. ''We've had a spate of some very bad luck in the last week or so.''

Interested, Rafe echoed, ''Bad luck?''

Megan nodded. ''We've had a fire break out in the basement. Fortunately one of the men saw it before it got out of hand. There's also been a ruptured water pipe. The damage caused by that was more extensive, but it was in the unoccupied wing of the clinic.'' That had led her to believe that both occurrences had somehow been orchestrated, although she had no idea to what end. Who would profit from the clinic's misfortunes? "On the minor side, things have been disappearing from the construction site with a fair amount of regularity. R.J. is having security beefed up." As president of the clinic, her son had already hired several extra people to patrol the area. "I really hope that discourages whoever's behind this." Although, if it was being orchestrated, she knew it would take more than just a few extra people patrolling the grounds to call a halt to the "accidents."

Greer slanted a look toward Rafe. She couldn't help wondering if perhaps his oldest sister was behind this somehow. There was some very bad blood between Janelle and the rest of the family. Charged with kidnapping and sent to prison to await trial, Janelle had managed to trick a guard and escape. No one knew where she was now. Was this her twisted way of exacting revenge on the Maitlands?

Greer could see by the way Rafe's expression sobered as he listened to Megan that he was thinking the same thing she was.

"If R.J. needs any more people, I'd like to volunteer to help out on the construction site, maybe keep my eyes and ears open, see what there is to see."

Stepping away from the doorway for a moment, Megan smiled at him gratefully. She knew she'd judged him correctly, despite Hugh's words of caution. Hugh worried too much.

"I appreciate the offer, but this is supposed to be your vacation, Rafe."

He'd just about had his fill of "vacationing." "I don't sit on my...backside—" about to say butt, he amended the word in deference to his aunt "—too well. He—ck, I'd welcome the chance to do something useful instead of just twiddling my thumbs."

Delighted, Megan laughed. "You don't have to keep censoring yourself on my account, Rafe. I've been around working men all my life and have heard just about everything." But she did like the fact that he made an effort to curb his language. A man who would do that was a man who knew how to treat a lady. "And I'm sure that R.J. would be grateful for the added eyes and ears. Nothing like having family involved." She winked. "I'll get that letter ready right away."

And with that promise, Megan withdrew.

"That was very nice of you to make the offer," Greer commented.

She was annoyed with herself for being so wrapped up in her own situation that she hadn't been aware of the accidents—not that she believed for a minute that they were accidents, not from the sound of it and certainly not in such abundance.

Besides, she didn't believe in luck. For the most

part, people created their own luck, and she firmly believed that someone was actively creating this so-called spate of bad luck for the Maitlands.

But why?

Rafe shrugged away the compliment. "If I don't start doing something soon, I'm going to go stir-crazy." Glancing over his shoulder, he stopped talking. People were passing by in the hallway. He didn't want anyone overhearing. He crossed to the door and closed it, then returned to Greer. "Are you still all right with this?" he asked, indicating the summons he'd brought.

She took it from him and perused it quickly, then refolded it and handed it back to him. This was nothing new.

"Sure, why wouldn't I be?"

He'd been giving the matter serious thought and was beginning to have second thoughts about the charade, especially with Megan offering to lend her support as well as her lawyer. Things might not go as well as he hoped they would if Greer had to testify.

"A woman of your moral fiber might choke at lying to a judge."

Greer looked down at the engagement ring he'd given her. It hadn't been off her finger since he had slipped it on.

"What lying?" she asked. "This is an engagement ring and you gave it to me.'' She raised her eyes to his, a touch of humor entering. ''That's usually the definition of *engagement,* isn't it?''

For the first time since he'd entered the room, Rafe smiled. Watching his mouth curve caused tidal waves to begin in her stomach, but she refrained from pressing her hand there in what she knew he'd probably view as an adolescent fashion.

But whether she pressed her hand there or not, the reaction continued.

As if reading her mind, he widened his smile. ''You are a constant source of surprise to me, Greer.''

This was the first time she had heard Rafe say her name without the usual note of amusement attached to it. ''Why?''

He crossed his arms before him, his eyes slowly traveling the length of her body. She felt herself growing warmer by the moment. ''Because to look at you, I'd say you were a straight arrow.''

She took a chance and guessed that this was a compliment in his book. ''I am.''

But he shook his head in response. ''Straight arrows don't know how to bend something so that it sounds like the truth when it isn't.''

She was acutely aware that it wasn't the truth—and that she was beginning to seriously want it to be.

A myriad of memories crowded her mind. Greer banked them all down. This wasn't the time.

"Maybe straight arrows have to learn how to bend things in order to survive," she countered.

There was something in her eyes, a sadness just then that spoke to him. Moved him so that, just for a second, he felt as if they were kindred spirits. Lies of necessity had been part of his life, as well, and he knew all too well what it was like not to want to lie, but to have no choice. After a while, it had become second nature to him.

Had it ever become second nature to her? Somehow, he doubted it. As he'd gotten to know her a little better, he realized there was a kind of nobility about her that would have prohibited her from sinking to that level.

"I know what you mean," he murmured, splaying his fingers along the side of her throat as he tilted her face up to his.

He found himself caught up in her eyes. Again. Warm brown eyes the color of deep, rich milk chocolate. He was suddenly wrestling with a craving for chocolate.

Before he could think to stop himself, Rafe touched his lips to hers. He felt her breath as she drew it in, felt her yielding as he allowed the kiss to linger on her lips. He had to hold himself in check to keep from getting carried away. It was becoming a definite possibility, he knew, and this wasn't the place for it.

Besides, he didn't want her to think he was taking advantage of the situation, even though he felt he was—and wanted to take further advantage of it because there was something about Greer that stirred him despite the fact that he had been with women who were far more glamorous.

He couldn't put his finger on what it was about Greer that momentarily separated him from his thoughts, his plans, and set him on a different path than the one he wanted to travel. He figured there was no point in trying to puzzle it out. After all, she wouldn't be part of his life that much longer. Just until after the holidays. Better just to enjoy it and to move on.

Eventually.

Chapter 10

At first Greer thought the noise was just the thudding of her heart as it slammed against her rib cage. Either that, or the rushing in her ears had gone up another notch and now seemed to be rattling everything around her, as well. Certainly it felt as if everything within her had shaken loose in the wake of the emotional earthquake she was experiencing.

Every time Rafe kissed her, she became more aware that there was a huge part of life she had been missing all these years. And it made her yearn to find a way somehow to claim it, if just for a little while. She'd never been intimate with a man, had never even wanted to be. There'd never been anyone in her life to arouse her passions, to make her want to take that risk. To invest her heart.

Sure, there'd been fantasies, but they were only that. Fantasies. And fantasies were by definition safe. She risked nothing.

But Rafe Maitland wasn't a fantasy. He was flesh and blood and very real. And she wanted him. Wanted him in the worst way. Wanted him to want her.

Wanted him to make love with her.

The noise came again and, slowly, Greer realized that the noise was real and not just a by-product of her body coming undone.

"Someone's knocking," she murmured, vaguely surprised that her lips still worked and could form intelligible words. They felt swollen from the pressure of his. Swollen had never felt so wonderful.

Rafe nodded, then as an afterthought released her, experiencing more than a shade of regret. He still wasn't sure just what it was that was going on here. Lord knew he'd kissed and been kissed by more than his share of women. Sexy women. Women who had been around and who knew the score. This almost completely clueless woman who'd lassoed his fancy was a virgin, he'd stake his life on it.

Maybe that was it, maybe he just wanted to be the first one. Rafe dismissed the thought the moment it occurred to him. Gathering trophies had never even remotely been his hang-up. He didn't believe in it, didn't see any reason to have something just to have it.

There was something else at play here. And not knowing what was beginning to eat at him.

"Right," he muttered, annoyed that he was so out of sync. Stepping back from her, he shoved his hands into his pockets, feeling oddly disembodied and trying hard not to look it. He nodded at the door. "Aren't you going to say 'come in'?"

Of course that's what she should be saying. Rafe had completely disoriented her. Again. It was beginning to happen with a fair amount of regularity. She was going to have to do something about that.

Greer more than half expected him to look amused, but Rafe appeared almost as bewitched, as bothered and bewildered as she felt.

Had to be her eyes, she decided. She was seeing things. A man like Rafe Maitland didn't *get* rattled, he rattled. And he had rattled her but good.

Greer ran her tongue along her lower lip before she said, "Come in?"

She upbraided herself for the uncertain way that had come out, but right now she wasn't even sure of her own name. The only thing she was sure of was that she loved this sensation racing through her and wished with all her heart that it could be allowed to continue.

But she better than anyone knew that was utterly impossible. Men like Rafe didn't fall for women like her. They didn't even stumble.

A petite, vibrant-looking blonde popped her head in as she opened the door to Greer's office. As bright as the burst of sunshine that Greer was even now still experiencing within her, the woman flashed a wide, knowing smile at both of them. Waltzing in, she left the door open, as if planning on a quick escape if things became too messy.

"Ah, just the two people I wanted to see. Rafe Maitland and Greer Lawford, right?" Her expression indicated that she wasn't really searching for confirmation. She already knew who they were.

"Right," Greer answered guardedly, gathering her bearings as she watched the other woman's face. She had absolutely no idea who this woman was or why she had come into her office looking for both of them. Other than the pseudo-engagement, there was no link between her and Rafe.

The engagement.

Oh, God, this wasn't someone from the society page, was it, she worried, here to do a story on another Maitland marriage in the works? The media was always hungry for any kind of news, good or bad, Greer thought uneasily. What if this woman was a reporter, here to ferret out a story about the wedding?

Rafe looked at the intruder suspiciously. Because he'd been addressed as well, he figured that gave him a right to a piece of the conversation. "We know who we are, the question here is, who are you?"

"Blossom Woodward." Blossom stuck her hand out. She shook first Rafe's hand, then Greer's. "So, does the happy couple intend to invite the rest of the family to the nuptials?"

She'd been right, Greer thought with dismay, this *was* a reporter. The woman's smile grew just a shade deeper and more eager. She made Greer think of a puppy on the scent of a treat.

Blossom turned her eyes and her charm on Rafe. "Like big brother, Luke, perhaps?"

Rafe's eyes narrowed, growing darker than thunder. "Who the hell are you?" he demanded.

Instantly, Greer went into damage control mode and moved forward. Rafe looked as if he was going to erupt right there in the office. The last thing she wanted was for him to come off badly in front of a reporter. The media could be exceptionally cruel and she didn't want the kind of repercussions that could arise, not for Rafe or for Mrs. Maitland.

"More to the point," she said to Blossom, "who sent you?"

Believing that discretion was the better part of valor, Blossom was deliberately vague.

"I'm a reporter," she began with the air of someone who was ready to roll right over any protest.

Greer continued to take her cue from the expression on Rafe's face. Though he'd only told her summarily that he had no idea where any of his family was, he hadn't made any particular comment about his older brother or the latter's whereabouts. That a reporter was trying to pump them for information in an utterly unsubtle manner only meant that there was some reason for Luke Maitland's being singled out.

Greer felt that people deserved their privacy, most of all those who were in the limelight. And, like it or not, because of his family ties, ties she was partially responsible for unearthing, Rafe was now in the limelight. She owed him this.

Her voice was slightly frosty as she told Blossom, "I believe the official statement is 'No comment.'"

The expression on the other woman's face was shrewd. "What's the unofficial one?"

"Same thing," Greer fired off.

"Is there any truth to the rumor that he's in the witness protection program because he was a witness to the assassination of Senator—?'' Blossom didn't get a chance to finish.

"Sorry, Ms. Woodward, but I'm afraid we're going to have to stick by 'no comment.'" Hooking her hand through the woman's arm, Greer abruptly drew Blossom over to the open doorway.

"But you do know where he is?" Blossom pressed Rafe even as she was being hustled out of the office.

"What do you think?" was all Greer enigmatically answered before she shut the door in the woman's face. Greer heard the latter loudly protest her ousting, citing freedom of the press and the First Amendment. "I'd seriously think about leaving now, Ms. Woodward, unless you'd like to be strong-armed by our security guards and escorted off the premises."

There was no reply. As she listened, Greer heard the sound of retreating footsteps.

Done.

Leaning against the door for a moment, Greer glanced at Rafe and saw that he was studying her and looked vaguely amused. "What?"

He'd been right. You really couldn't judge a book by its cover, he thought. "You can be a real ball of fire when you want to be, can't you?"

The light in his eyes warmed her. "It's my job

to screen these kinds of annoyances and stop them before they get in the faces of the people who…''

Her voice trailed off as Greer realized that she wasn't entirely making any sense or even sure what she was saying. But that was his fault. He was looking at her like that again. As if she was pretty. As if she was desirable. She wished he'd stop.

She wished he'd keep on doing that forever.

She figured only the first wish was doable.

Struggling for a degree of composure, she pointed out, ''You're smiling. Why?''

He was smiling because he got a kick out of the way she seemed to shed her uncertain demeanor and suddenly became a defender, but he decided that saying any more on the subject would only embarrass her further.

''Nothing, it's just that I finally met someone with a name sillier than yours.'' He shook his head. ''Greer, Blossom. Doesn't anyone out here have a normal name?''

She'd never really cared for her name, but it was the only thing that was actually hers. Even her last name didn't belong to her. It belonged to some actor who had been famous in the forties and fifties. She'd selected it late one night while watching an old movie on television when she was seventeen.

''Normal,'' Greer echoed. ''You mean like Hannah or Sara?''

Rafe inclined his head, playing along. "For starters. Fine, upstanding names."

She wasn't about to argue the point. They had been the first names that had popped into her head. They'd belonged to two girls who had been with her at the orphanage. Two girls who had gotten adopted while she hadn't. She'd hated Sara and Hannah.

Returning to her desk, she began to straighten the already tidy objects on its surface just to have something to do with her hands.

"Well, I don't know about 'Blossom,' but I'm lucky my mother didn't just call me 'hey you,' or tag a number to me."

Compassion stirred within him. He hadn't meant to drag up any painful memories for her, he'd only been trying to tease her.

"Sorry, I guess I stuck my foot in it, didn't I?" He tried to shift the mood. "And after you were so feisty and all."

It was a silly word. Why did it make her feel like preening? She couldn't help the smile that curved her lips. "Feisty, me?"

He liked watching the way a smile seemed to light up her whole face.

"Feisty, you," Rafe emphasized. "Weren't you listening? I was." He'd been sure that the other woman was about to steamroll right over her. That

Greer had not only stood up to her but pushed her out of the office had been a complete surprise. "What I heard was pretty damn good. But you were too easy on her."

She knew he meant that she should have called Security immediately and had the woman forcibly removed. Greer shrugged. "Maybe. But she has to make a living, too, I guess."

That was no excuse in his book. "She could try doing something respectable instead of invading people's lives." Rafe rocked back on his heels for a minute, studying her face. In his experience, there was nothing more curious than a woman who'd been given just a small scrap of information to tantalize her, yet Greer had said nothing. "Aren't you going to ask me?"

Greer tucked the folders she'd been pretending to peruse between the two cherubic bookends that resided on her desk. "Ask you what?"

The reporter had been hot to know where his brother was. He had no idea what she was talking about when she'd mentioned the witness protection program. Probably just a figment of the woman's imagination. Still, Greer didn't know for certain if he knew anything or not. Any other woman would have been prodding him by now.

"If I know where Luke is."

Greer began to shrug again, then caught herself.

"I already asked you that and you said you didn't know where any of your family was currently. There's no reason for me to think that you were withholding information."

She'd said "withholding information" instead of lying. The woman knew how to tiptoe around words when she wanted to, he thought, amused. "Aren't you the least bit curious about why someone like this Flower—"

"Blossom," she corrected him, a grin tugging at the corners of her mouth.

A sudden urge to run his thumb along her smile and seal it to her lips came out of nowhere. He chose not to explore it for the time being. "Whatever—is really looking for Luke?"

Ordinarily, she didn't give people like Blossom any thought. To her, reporters who worked for tabloids and tabloid television were nothing less than marauders, looking for a morsel of a story and ready to ruin anyone's life to get it. Yes, the woman had to make a living as she'd pointed out to Rafe, but Blossom Woodward, or her kind, didn't have to do it on her time.

"That 'witness protection program' angle is probably some trumped-up lead-in on her third-rate show used to get people to tune in. More than likely, it'll be forgotten once the program gets under way."

Did she know the woman by reputation? Did watching that kind of program come under the heading of a guilty pleasure for Greer? His curiosity aroused, Rafe leaned a hip on the corner of her desk. "How do you know it's third-rate?"

"Because first-rate news programs don't deal in shady sensationalism and I've got a feeling that little Miss Blossom does."

And, since the woman had both a face and a figure that left a lasting impression on the male mind, Greer judged that Blossom probably managed to "break" a great many stories. Whether they were true or not was another matter entirely.

Greer wondered if Blossom had managed to intrigue Rafe despite what she represented. She was certainly gorgeous enough for that. Suddenly, Greer didn't feel like discussing the woman any longer. With a knack honed across the boardroom table, she changed the topic.

She put out her hand. "Now, let me see that summons again so I can jot down the date and arrange my calendar accordingly."

He pulled the envelope out of his back pocket and gave it to her. Greer made the necessary notations on her oversize desk calendar and then handed the summons back to him.

That done, she asked, "Anything else?" and hoped she didn't sound too eager. What she'd hoped for when she saw him in the doorway was that he'd come to take her to lunch again. Though it had only happened a few times, she'd already gotten used to taking her meals with him.

Just as she had already gotten accustomed to having him in her life. She knew the danger in that, but it was already too late to attempt to shore up her beaches. He'd landed on them and planted his flag. If she'd had any doubts about it, the last kiss had shown her just how vulnerable she was.

And how taken with him.

"Yeah." He tucked the summons into his back pocket again. "Where do I go to find R.J.?"

She tried to hide her disappointment. "You were serious about volunteering to do security work?"

He'd been giving the matter some thought ever since Megan had mentioned the accidents and decided that it wouldn't hurt to help out. One job was as good as another and it might as well be something where he could do some good. Besides, if Megan was going to throw her support behind him in the custody battle, he felt as if he owed her something in return. This was small-enough a payment.

"I was serious about going stir-crazy," he answered. "There're just so many games of pattycake a man can be expected to play."

She grinned again. He had to be pulling her leg or exaggerating. Though she had seen him with

Bethany, try as she might Greer couldn't begin to imagine him clapping his hands and then hitting those same large, callused hands against a set of tiny ones.

"Patty-cake?"

He realized he'd made a tactical error in his admission and there was no way off this ice floe. He shrugged, looking off.

"Gotta teach her something and I don't know any good stories or games."

Uncomfortable, he opened the door to see if Blossom was lurking somewhere in the hallway.

But the woman was gone.

Leaning on the doorknob, Rafe looked back at Greer. "So, where can I find him?"

Reluctant to have him leave, she stepped out into the hall. Very succinctly, she gave him directions to his older brother's first-floor office. "I can take you there if you like."

But he shook his head. "No, you've got work to do."

"It'll keep."

Her own answer surprised her. But her next train of thought surprised her even more. It wasn't often that she gave in to impulse and Greer had never thought of herself as impetuous, but something prompted her to make a suggestion that, for all intents and purposes, was evidence that her brain had disengaged itself.

"Rafe, I'm sure everything's going to be fine at the hearing." She paused to run the tip of her tongue along lips that had suddenly become very dry. She saw him silently watching her, obviously wondering where she was going with this. It was now or never. "But if you think it might help…" Her courage flagged.

Waiting, Rafe prompted, "Yes?" when she didn't follow up with anything.

Damn it, she shouldn't have started this, Greer upbraided herself. Swallowing, she had no choice but to finish.

"If you think it might help," she began again, "to keep Bethany, I mean, I'm willing to go through a wedding ceremony."

The phrasing was nothing short of awkward. He'd learned enough about Greer to know that wasn't like her. The offer caught him completely off guard.

"You mean marry me?"

Unable to force the words out of her mouth, struggling hard not to grow crimson because of what she'd just said, Greer could only nod her head like some puppeteer's marionette.

She looked scared to death that he'd take her up on that, Rafe thought. Touched by the offer, he took her hand in his. Funny how he hadn't realized before now how delicate it felt.

He tried to ease her fears as best he could. "Not that I'm not grateful for the offer, Greer, but I don't think that'll be necessary."

Meaning that not even his fierce desire to hang on to Bethany would force him to make such a huge sacrifice as marrying her, she thought. Why should he? Look at him. Look at her. What had she been thinking?

Even so, the realization that he wouldn't want her under any circumstances stung. A great deal. She was vaguely aware of drawing her hand away. And more than vaguely aware that she suddenly wanted to lay her head down on her desk and sob her heart out.

Because she'd always managed to get up no matter how often fate had knocked her down and robbed her of her hopes, she managed to rally. "Just thought I'd cover all the bases," she murmured.

He accepted the remark at face value, wondering if that was relief he saw in her eyes or something else.

"I think they're covered," he assured. "Thanks for the directions." With that, he left.

Numbly, she ran her thumb over her engagement

ring, staring at Rafe's back as he disappeared down the hall.

Damn it, why couldn't she just leave well enough alone? Why did she insist, now of all times, on suddenly trying to take something further, to push her way into a place where there was a definite No Admittance sign posted along with the words "This means you, Greer" inscribed beneath it?

Because she'd gotten carried away.

Because like the egotistical actor who'd been created by his publicist, she'd gotten to believe her own press. In this case, the press had to do with the way both she and Rafe had been pretending to be engaged. To be in love. One of them wasn't pretending.

She held back a sob that was suddenly clawing at her throat. He'd kissed her while no one was watching, in an office whose door was closed. Wasn't that supposed to mean something?

Didn't it?

It didn't.

She was her worst enemy, finding the answer to every hopeful protest she made. All his kissing her just then meant was that Rafe had climbed into his character and felt it best to remain there so that he would be believable when others were around. If someone had walked in on the kiss just then, it would have been that much better for his case.

The pretense, kissing her, saying nice things to her, all that meant less than nothing to him.

But not to her.

For her it had aroused every dormant emotion she possessed, every dormant emotion she had tried so hard to convince herself no longer existed.

Except that they did.

Well, that was her problem, not his, Greer told herself. One that she was determined to ignore until it went away of its own accord.

The more pressing problem, one that she wasn't about to ignore, was finding a way to get all of her work done or delegated so that she could be at his side when the all-important hearing took place.

She looked down at the engagement ring on her finger. Sunlight, which shone through the window at her back, grazed it, shooting out streams of rainbows. Fascinated, she moved her hand up and down for a moment, watching the beams of light play off the walls.

It's only on loan, it's not yours. Don't get used to it.

But she could pretend. Pretend the ring and the man were hers. Just for now. Just to be convincing.

But did she need to be? If Mrs. Maitland was going to send her lawyer to the hearing and a statement to the effect that she fully supported Rafe in his efforts to gain custody, if Rafe had the serious backing of the head of the Maitland family, why on earth did he still need her?

The answer was that he didn't.

She knew it was just a matter of time before the same thought occurred to him, too. And then Cinderella would have to return to the hearth to tend to her daydreams.

Greer sighed as the thought sank in.

There'd be no castles in the sky for her, no prince waiting with open arms once the story was over. For one thing, she had no fairy godmother waiting in the wings with a magic wand to transform her from the plain woman she was into something a man like Rafe Maitland would find desirable.

She had no business dabbling in daydreams, or any other kind of dreams, for that matter. She had no place in the "what might be." What she had to do was stick to what she knew and was good at.

Another sigh escaped her as she returned to reviewing her schedule for the coming month. Maybe he wouldn't realize that he really didn't need her until the hearing was over. She crossed her fingers as she turned the page.

Chapter 11

There was no answer to her knock. Wondering if something was wrong, Greer tried the doorknob and found that it gave under her hand. She hesitated for a moment, then opened the door and stepped slowly into the guesthouse.

She didn't ordinarily invade anyone else's space, but then, she didn't ordinarily feel this way, either. Ever since Rafe had come into her life, or she had come into his, depending on your view of things, she thought, her life had been slightly off kilter.

Something kept her from calling out Rafe's name. Instead, she quietly made her way into the living room.

It was very early. Their flight to Nevada took off in approximately two hours, but she liked getting to the airport in plenty of time. In the interest of speed, she had offered to come and pick Rafe and Bethany up at the estate, after which the chauffeur would drive all three of them to the airport. They were to meet Hugh Blake, Mrs. Maitland's lawyer, at the appropriate terminal and fly back for the hearing together.

Rafe was in the living room, dressed in the suit she'd selected for him that first day when he'd met his family. He looked more handsome than anyone had a right to be, Greer thought. He was sitting on the edge of the sofa, Bethany on his lap, seemingly oblivious to the presence of anyone else in the room.

He was talking to the little girl, and Greer stopped to listen before letting him know she was in the room.

"This is it, kid, this is for all the marbles. But I don't want you to worry. It's going to be all right." He looked at Bethany very seriously. "I don't break promises and I swear I won't break this one."

They were pressed for time and Austin traffic wasn't always the friendliest, otherwise, Greer would have withdrawn without letting him know that she'd intruded on his moment. Instead, she cleared her throat to get his attention. When he glanced her way, she asked, "Didn't you hear me knock?"

"I heard."

"Then why didn't you answer?"

He continued looking at Bethany, trying to absorb everything about the toddler in case the worst happened and he was forced to break his word.

"I just wanted a few more minutes with her." He looked up at Greer. "I've been sitting here, trying to imagine what it would be like, not having her to hold, and I can't. I just can't."

His expression tugged at her heart. This had to come out right, it had to. If there was any justice in heaven, it had to.

"Then don't," she told him passionately. Without stopping to censor her actions, she placed her hand on his shoulder. "It's going to be all right."

Rafe reached up, placing his own hand over hers. He was the one who was supposed to say that, he thought. He'd been saying it all of his life, riding over the bumps that came in the road, picking his way through the brambles. And now he was the one who suddenly needed reassurance. He couldn't believe that such a pint-size little creature could reduce him to someone who was so vulnerable.

"Yeah, right." His voice was gruff to cover the discomfort he felt at being momentarily needy. Rafe got to his feet. "Let's get this over with."

Greer retreated, striving to become all-business again, which was getting harder and harder to do around Rafe.

"The sooner we do, the sooner you'll be able to go on with the rest of your life. Lives," she corrected him, looking at Bethany.

Rafe merely nodded as he walked to the door. Greer fell into step beside him.

Feelings. It all came down to feelings, Greer decided late that afternoon as she watched the judge presiding over Rafe's case.

If the judge trying the case felt kindly toward them, then Rafe would win the little girl he'd come to love as his own. If the judge felt strongly about such things as traditions and bloodlines, then Bethany, whom they'd left waiting out in the hall with Alyssa, would be going home with Lil Butler's aunt and uncle instead of Rafe at the end of the hearing.

Greer didn't know if she could stand much more of this.

Rafe was so attached to the little girl, losing custody would irreparably scar him. It was as if the little girl had brought out everything that was good within him, everything he'd stored up during the stormy childhood he had told her about. Losing Bethany might not kill him, but it would come damn close. She would do anything to prevent that.

She'd come to feel very protective of him, she realized. The thought made her smile to herself. There was no doubt in her mind that Rafe would probably laugh out loud if he knew how she felt. It didn't change anything, though. She still wanted to make the trial come out right.

The silence within the courtroom as the judge deliberated over the last point that had been raised was swiftly driving her crazy. If it was doing that to her, what must it be doing to Rafe?

She slanted a look toward him. His face was tense, rigid.

Without thinking, Greer slipped her hand over his. As if suddenly aware of her presence, Rafe looked at her and then slowly smiled.

He probably thought she'd added that touch to show the judge a united front, Greer mused. The thought had only occurred to her after the fact. She'd just wanted to touch Rafe's hand, to mutely communicate her feelings and her support to him.

As if that meant anything, she mocked herself. But her hand remained where it was.

''Ms. Lawford.''

Greer's eyes darted toward the judge as she spoke her name, her heart accelerating. Belatedly, she pulled her hand back.

''Tell me,'' the judge continued, ''just what does

a thirty-year-old dedicated career woman know about motherhood?''

The judge's tone of voice clearly said ''convince me'' to her. She saw Mrs. Maitland's lawyer begin to rise in protest. Greer sprang to her feet, her hands braced on the table for support, praying she wouldn't trip on her own tongue.

It's business, she told herself urgently, *think business.*

''Nothing.''

The answer took the judge by surprise. After a moment, the judge cleared her throat. ''Well, then, perhaps—''

''But what does any woman really know about motherhood before she has a baby?'' Greer quickly followed up. ''Yes, there are books to read and friends to talk to, but I can do that as well as any other woman. Not having given birth to Bethany doesn't automatically knock me out of the running, Your Honor. The fact that I'm a businesswoman shows that I can stick to a job and see it through.''

There was no indication on the judge's face as to whether she was making her point or not. It remained impassive. ''Is that how you view motherhood?'' she asked curiously. ''As a job?''

That had been an unfortunate choice of words. Greer knew the logical thing was to retract her statement, but that wouldn't be coming from a position of strength and she had a feeling that the judge respected strength. So she pressed on, turning a minus into a plus.

"At times. Being a mother means having schedules and deadlines and things that absolutely have to be attended to right away, just like any job." She thought of the new wing being added to the clinic. "Whether it's construction work or running the country, or being a mother, there is a great deal of job frustration when things aren't going right and extreme job satisfaction when they are." She remembered what it felt like, holding Bethany in her arms and having the little girl recognize her and cuddle against her. "And personally, Your Honor, I can't think of anything more rewarding than the job of being Bethany's mother."

The judge scrutinized her as closely as if she'd had her on a slide under a microscope. "So you believe you'll be a good mother—"

This time Hugh Blake gained his feet. "Your Honor, we're talking of granting custody to Mr. Maitland," he protested, "not Ms. Lawford."

The judge looked at him sternly. "Yes, but Mr. Maitland is marrying Ms. Lawford." She looked from one table to the other. "On the one hand, we already have a family unit. Mr. and Mrs. Preston have been married for a great many years, have raised their late niece, who I am told was a fine young woman..."

It was on the tip of Rafe's tongue to protest that Lil's character had evolved despite the cold couple sitting to the right of him, not because of them, but he managed to keep his silence. Outbursts would only make him seem hot-tempered and work against him. Right or wrong, for some reason the brunt of the case seemed to be riding on the shoulders of the woman he'd capriciously challenged to join forces with him.

Rafe fervently hoped he wouldn't live to regret the act.

"Yes," Greer replied with feeling.

The judge raised a brow. "Yes?" she echoed.

"Yes, I will make a good mother," Greer clarified for the older woman.

Though she hated baring her feelings, her past, especially in front of strangers, this really wasn't about her. This was about a little girl who needed Rafe, and Rafe who needed the little girl. Dwelling on that helped ease her through her discomfort.

"I will make a very good mother because I have all this love stored up inside of me. Love I haven't begun to use yet." Greer drew herself up a tad, as if to withstand blows from some invisible hand. "I was an orphan, Your Honor, and I always swore that any child I had would never go through what

I did. They would never know a moment when they didn't feel loved and cared for."

The judge looked at her thoughtfully. "I see."

The black-robed woman paused again, looking down at the statement that Megan Maitland's lawyer had previously submitted to her. That alone carried a great deal of weight. Mrs. Maitland's reputation as a humanitarian preceded her.

But ultimately, it would be the young couple's responsibility to see to the child's welfare, not Megan Maitland's. The judge wanted to make sure she wasn't being unduly swayed.

"As I was saying, on the one side—" she looked at Lil's aunt and uncle "—we have the right of family. Tradition, stability. On the other, we have an untried, as of yet unwed couple. We have promises. We have youth." A hint of a smile emerged. "And from what I can see, we have love and passion."

"Your Honor," Will Preston complained, struggling to his feet, "Mildred and I've been married for over thirty years, you can't expect us to exude passion—"

The hint widened until it took over the judge's entire face. "I was referring to the passionate way Ms. Lawford spoke just now. About the love she has for this child who is not hers, at least not yet in the eyes of the law. But soon." She smiled at

Greer. "I have always been a great fan of youth
and promise." Judge Winfield brought down her
gavel decisively. "I rule in favor of Mr. Maitland.
As per her parents' expressed wishes, he is hereby
granted custody of one Bethany Butler." The
judge's voice lost some of its official distance. "I
would like to see you back in my courtroom in six
months, Mr. Maitland, so you and your new wife
can tell me then just how things are going." She
rose, an imposing, towering figure in black standing
well over six feet. "By the way, give my regards
to your aunt. Court's adjourned."

"Your Honor, I protest," the Prestons' lawyer
declared, jumping to his feet.

Judge Winfield paused on her way out. "That is
your right, Mr. Saunders. Protest all you want, this
is a free and glorious country we live in. Good day,
sir." With a sweep of her robe, she was gone.

"We did it." Rafe uttered the words in quiet
awe. He'd hoped, prayed, but part of him, the part
that had grown up getting hard knocks, hadn't really believed it would go his way. "You did it!"
he declared with verve, as the realization finally
sank in and found a home within his chest. He re-
sisted the temptation to sweep Greer up in his arms
and swing her around.

Greer's heart leaped up, spurred by the look she
saw in his eyes. They were smiling at her. *He* was

smiling at her. The next moment, she found herself being caught in a huge embrace. Adrenaline rushed through her in euphoric excitement.

She saw Hugh Blake looking at her over Rafe's shoulder. The older man nodded his approval.

"Nicely done."

"You haven't heard the last of this," the Prestons' lawyer warned as he came to their table. His briefcase hit the tabletop for emphasis.

"Perhaps we have," Hugh responded mildly, unfazed. He snapped his briefcase closed as the bailiff left the courtroom. Picking it up, he spared the Prestons a glance before looking at Saunders. "Mrs. Maitland has authorized me to cut a check for your clients with the firm understanding that while they may visit Bethany with the approval of Mr. Maitland," he stipulated, "they will sign an agreement giving up their claim to Bethany's custody once and for all."

Saunders withdrew for a moment to discuss the offer with his clients, then turned and looked at Hugh. "How much?"

The eternally popular phrase, Hugh thought. They'd won hands down. He knew they would. Megan, he knew, would be very pleased. And if she was, he was.

"Let's discuss the particulars over lunch, shall we?" Herding the other man before him, Hugh turned back for a moment to look at the younger couple. "I think you can consider the matter settled." He shook Rafe's hand. "See you at the party."

"Party?" Rafe asked Greer as Hugh and the others crossed to the rear door.

She'd almost forgotten all about that. "Mrs. Maitland is giving a fund-raiser tomorrow night to raise more money for the completion of the new wing."

As always, she'd taken care of the details for the fund-raiser, the latest of many. But right now, wrapped in the warm arms of triumph, basking in Rafe's smile, it was hard for her to remember anything, hard to think at all.

"It completely slipped my mind." Her apology went without saying.

He nodded. "We both had more important things to think of."

Truer words had never been spoken. The late September sun was already withdrawing from the courtroom as she scrutinized his face. "But you'll go? Mrs. Maitland said she'd like to see you there."

He had no use for parties, and he would have rather turned down the invitation. But he owed his aunt a great deal. He believed in honoring his debts. If his attendance was important to Megan, his duty was clear.

"Then I'll be there." He looked at Greer significantly, well aware of what he owed her as well.
Granted, Megan's letter had paved the way for him,
but he had a feeling that Greer had tipped the scales
in his favor. "*We'll* be there."

She felt her heart singing even though she knew
it had no business even humming. This was all just
part of the ruse they were required to keep up just
a little longer. Just until the Prestons signed on the
dotted line and relinquished their claim to a child
they really didn't seem to want in the first place.

Maybe, she suddenly realized, this had been their
plan all along, to hold out for monetary compensation once they'd realized who Rafe was related
to.

The more she considered it, the more plausible it
sounded. The souls of some people were darker
than she liked to think.

But she was learning.

"Let's go. We've got a little girl to collect," he
said to her as he took her hand.

Greer let herself be taken away by the moment.

There was barely enough time to step out into
the hallway before a cameraman suddenly materialized, aiming his camera directly at them. Greer
recognized Blossom Woodward a second before the
woman pushed herself and a microphone into their
collective faces.

Instantly, Rafe went to shield Greer, pushing her behind him. "What the...?"

Blossom fairly bounced in front of him, the black magic wand that would propel his voice into virtually millions of homes held tightly in her hand. She pushed it up toward his face as she signaled the cameraman to approach even closer.

"Tell me, how does it feel to have enough money for the first time in your life to buy off the people who are posing a threat to you?"

For a second, Rafe could only stare at the blonde. "How the hell did you find that out?"

"Good investigative reporting," Blossom fairly crowed, proud of the lucky fluke that had allowed her to gain access to the material. There was no way she was going to divulge her source. Or have that source ridiculed.

Alyssa looked at them helplessly. "I'm sorry, they just popped out of nowhere a couple of minutes ago."

"Not your fault," Rafe said as Greer took the baby from Alyssa before he could. Using his body as a shield, he hustled both women past the cameraman. The man began to angle for a better shot. "Stick that thing into my face again, buddy, and I'm going to feed it to you piece by piece," he warned the man heatedly.

Rafe placed his back between the lens and the two women.

The elevator doors yawned open. There was no room to maneuver. The cameraman settled for the footage he'd already gotten. "You Maitlands are hard people to profile," Blossom called after him.

"Good!" Rafe shot back as he bit off fairly choice words better kept to himself.

He looked around carefully to see if he'd been followed. But there was no one along the small, tight corridor that ran beneath the new wing that was currently under construction. The construction workers had long since left and gone home.

He had his excuse in place if someone did spot him.

"Just checking things out before I knock off for the day. Never can be too careful, you know."

A smile peeled slowly along his lips. Yeah, he'd learned that lesson, all right. The hard way. But there wasn't going to be a hard way for him. Not any longer. He'd done his time in that cell, now he wanted something better. Could have something better.

All it took was careful planning and more careful execution. He figured he was up to it.

After all, the prize was a big one, an exclusive one. One that he'd had in his hands once before and stupidly let go. He wasn't going to make the same mistake twice.

He wasn't going to make a mistake at all.

Picking his way through the darkened corridor, he shone his flashlight on the pile of building materials stacked to the side. The ones to be used in the morning.

"Not tomorrow morning," he murmured under his breath. They'd have to get new ones once he was finished.

Carefully, he wiped his brow with the handkerchief he took out. The one with initials carefully stitched in one corner of the fine linen.

H.B.

Then, tossing it aside on the ground, he raised his lighter to the overhead sprinkling system that had just been put in place at the beginning of the week. Within seconds, a shower began.

He hurried from the corridor as the fire alarm went on. He knew a way out where security wouldn't be able to see him.

The smile on his lips was one of self-satisfaction.

"I hear you won."

Feeling slightly out of focus, like a monitor with misaligned horizontal and vertical hold buttons, Greer looked up from her desk to see Anna walking into her office.

Was there something she was supposed to be doing for Megan's daughter, as well?

This was the first chance she'd had to get at the work that had accumulated on her desk during the last twenty-four hours while she'd been in Nevada. She had just begun to sort through the various phone messages that had come in during her absence, and she was beginning to feel seriously overwhelmed and far from clearheaded.

Stopping, Greer rubbed the bridge of her nose. There was a headache threatening to erupt directly behind her eyes.

"Yes, we won, thanks to your mother and her generosity."

Anna parked herself on the edge of Greer's desk, studying the other woman intently. In her opinion Greer turned modesty into an art form.

"That's not the way Hugh tells it. He told Mother that the judge grilled you and you came through with flying colors. He thinks that Rafe is getting himself quite a prize." Leaning forward, she pressed Greer's hand in intimate camaraderie. "And he's right."

Blushing, embarrassed at the lie she was forced to keep alive, Greer shook her head. "Mr. Blake is being very kind."

"He's a kind man," Anna granted, "but above all a truthful one. That's why Mother's kept him on

all these years.'' That, and she was beginning to
suspect, because there was a spark between her
mother and the handsome attorney. ''I've never
known Hugh Blake not to tell it exactly as it is.''
It was time, Anna decided, to take the bull by the
horns and get down to the real reason she'd come
here looking for Greer. ''Speaking of the way
things are, I know you've been extremely busy
these last few weeks, but you need to take a little
time out to plan this wedding of yours.'' She could
have sworn she saw a flash of panic in Greer's eyes.
But it was gone the next moment. ''I don't even
have a date.''

For a second, she considered telling Anna the day
Rafe had mentioned, Valentine's Day. It was hopelessly romantic, but if she said that to Anna, Greer
knew the woman would be off and running in a
matter of moments. Rafe didn't need this added
complication.

Greer began shuffling papers again, this time
hardly seeing what was written on them. She
wished Anna would turn her attention to something
else. ''That's because we haven't really pinned one
down,'' she lied.

Anna's eyes narrowed slightly as she continued
studying Greer's face. ''Don't you think that maybe
you should?''

''Soon,'' Greer promised. ''Soon. But right

now—'' she grabbed the nearest folder and opened it ''—I need to get back to work.''

To Greer's surprise, Anna placed her hand against the folder and closed it for her.

"What you need to do is learn how to delegate," Anna corrected her. She cocked her head, her sharp eyes taking measure of the planes and angles of the slender face before her. "Tell me, have you ever thought of having a makeover?"

Nervous, uncertain, Greer began to feel as if she was under a microscope. She stalled, trying to think. "A what?"

"A makeover," Anna repeated patiently.

Anna's mind was already racing ahead. Most of the better salons in Austin were booked well in advance, but the Maitland name could be used to pry loose an appointment, especially if the word *emergency* was bandied about. And a few well-spent hours at Neiman Marcus with an experienced salesclerk wouldn't hurt, either, she decided. Greer dressed far too conservatively.

A makeover. Something they did with women who garnered other women's pity. Greer pressed her lips together, knowing that Anna hadn't meant to be hurtful. It wasn't Anna's fault she was an ugly duckling that had never managed to be transformed.

"You mean like those beauty things they do on daytime talk shows and women's magazines?"

"Yes." Anna placed a comforting hand gently on Greer's shoulder. "Don't knock it until you try it."

"I'm not knocking it," Greer protested. "But I really don't have to try it to know that it would be a waste of time."

"How so?" Anna crossed her arms before her, humor tugging at her lips. "Do you feel you've reached perfection?"

Greer laughed incredulously. The question was ludicrous. The word *perfection* didn't belong in the same sentence with her name.

"No. It's a waste of time because nobody can do anything to make me look any better."

And that, Greer hoped, was the end of it. She didn't need to go to some salon and have a man with a ponytail clucking over her as he shook his head and mumbled something like, "Well, at least her skin isn't a complete disaster."

"I do believe you're challenging me, Greer." Anna's eyes began to glow brightly. "And I do dearly love a challenge."

Oh, God, she'd gone and said the wrong thing. This was the last thing she wanted to do, to challenge Anna. Concerned, Greer tried vainly to backpedal.

"No, really, I didn't mean to challenge you, it's just that—" Helpless, she fell back on an old adage she'd heard applied to her more than once. She winced even to repeat it. "You know that saying about a silk purse and a sow's ear?"

The laughter faded from Anna's lips. "You're not going to tell me you think you're a sow's ear, are you? Greer, you get out of that chair this minute. The party's tonight and you and I have work to do."

Greer tried one more time. "Anna, I appreciate what you think you're going to do, but I am a plain woman, and when you finish, all you're going to have is a plain woman in expensive clothing and, likely as not, a silly hairdo. Believe me, I know my limitations—"

Anna was not about to take no for an answer. Once upon a time, someone had obviously done a very bad number on Greer and it apparently had a lasting effect. She wasn't about to let that go on any longer.

"Then you're the only one who does. Please, indulge me. You're a beautiful woman inside, it's time we did a little maximizing with what's on the outside, as well." She wasn't getting anywhere. Anna fixed Greer with a knowing look. "It's time you stopped hiding."

Greer hadn't a clue what Anna was talking about. "Hiding?"

"Uh-huh. It's very easy to say you didn't win

the race because you didn't run. Running takes courage. *Risking* losing takes courage."

That made nothing any clearer. "Am I supposed to understand this analogy?"

Anna smiled confidentially as she tucked her hand under Greer's elbow and coaxed her to her feet. She could call André at the salon from the car.

"It's enough that I do. Now, I'm the boss's daughter and the future bridegroom's sister, so don't give me any lip," she managed to say with a straight face before laughing.

Put that way, Greer had no choice but to go along. Besides, she reasoned, with any luck, Anna would tire of the game soon enough and give up.

Chapter 12

A frown creased Megan's lips as she let the receiver drop back into its cradle. Was she doing the right thing, stalling this way? Would the situation only get more uncomfortable if she did? Maybe it was best to have everything over with and out in the open.

She just wasn't sure. It was so hard to know if she was making the right decisions. Who said wisdom came with age? The only thing that came with age, she thought, were more questions.

"A penny for your thoughts."

At the sound of the soothing, familiar voice, her frown faded instantly. Turning from the writing ta-

ble where the old-fashioned phone was perched, she
saw that Harold had shown Hugh into the study.
Just seeing Hugh with his strong, distinguished
bearing gave her confidence.

She smiled up at him. "What, no adjustment for
inflation?"

Hugh crossed to her and took both her hands in
his. The quip he was about to say disappeared as
he looked in surprise at the woman he had known
and respected for so many years.

"Megan, your hands are like ice. What is it?"

"Poor circulation?" she suggested innocently,
hoping he wouldn't probe any further.

His expression told her no such luck. Hugh
wasn't about to be put off. "We've been together
far too long for you to hide things from me, Megan.
Come on, out with it. What's bothering you?"

She took her time in answering, carefully choos-
ing her words. She knew this was going to be as
much of a surprise to Hugh as it had initially been
to her. Over the years, Hugh had become far more
than just the family lawyer. She had come to rely
on him for so many things. For his humor, for his
wisdom and, most important of all, for his never-
failing support. Of late, there'd been something
more added to all this, a feeling that they might
come to mean more to each other, and she didn't

want to jeopardize it before it had a chance to develop.

Megan withdrew her hands from his. "Clyde Mitchum's turned up." She watched his face as he absorbed the news and saw disbelief imprint itself on Hugh's distinguished patrician features.

"What does he want?"

There was more than just a lawyer's indignation in his eyes. She took a breath before answering. "He wants me to arrange a meeting between him and Connor."

Hugh caught himself, getting his feelings under control before they could fully surface. He had always prided himself on his poker face. It often came in handy in the courtroom. But it was harder to exercise that ability around a woman he had come to care for so deeply. "Mitchum? Are you sure? I thought he was dead." Hoped, really, he added silently.

"So did I."

Megan sighed, feeling suddenly very weary. That had been Clyde on the phone just now. He'd wanted to come to the fund-raiser, knowing that Connor and his wife would be there. She'd told him no in no uncertain terms, but that didn't alleviate the doubts that refused to be assuaged.

"But ghosts don't know how to work telephones." She saw the slight line of concern form-

ing on Hugh's brow just above the bridge of his
nose, saw his jaw tightening as he struggled for the
control she knew he was so proud of. "He came to
see me a few weeks ago, out of the blue after all
these years. He told me that he wanted to make
amends, that he was a changed man—"

Alarms went off all through Hugh's head.
"Don't trust him, Megan."

A fond smile played on her lips. She would have
expected nothing less from Hugh. "Is that the lawyer talking, or the old friend?"

Hugh took her hand in his again, looking into her
eyes. Remembering how long he had been waiting
for her. And how he would continue to wait, until
she was ready. He didn't want to take a chance on
someone from her past ruining everything.

"Both."

Her smile widened and reached her eyes. "Then
I'll take it under advisement."

She was her own woman and he cared very
deeply for her. To attempt to take things out of her
hands would be to insult her and he wouldn't do
that for all the world. That tied his own hands in a
way he wasn't happy about.

He tried to divert their attention to something
lighter.

"In the meantime, you have a whole host of
guests arriving in your ballroom, their wallets bulg-

ing with money they need to get rid of." His eyes twinkling, he presented his arm to her. "Shall we?" Megan threaded her arm through his and he led her to the doorway. "By the way, did I tell you how lovely you look tonight?"

Megan laughed softly as they entered the hall. "Not yet, but go ahead. I think I'd like to hear it right about now."

He didn't disappoint her.

Greer felt nervousness skitter through her.

Anna hadn't let her go home to change. Instead, she had insisted on sequestering her here inside the mansion to prepare for the fund-raiser. When Greer had protested that there were still a thousand details to see to for that very fund-raiser, Anna had effectively parried her objections and said that everything was being taken care of.

The only thing Anna had allowed her to retrieve from her own apartment were her contact lenses. She'd ordered them in a moment of vanity, gone through the rigors of getting herself accustomed to them and then decided they were too much trouble to bother with in the morning. Anna had made her promise to leave her glasses in the room.

It had seemed like fun earlier, being whisked through Neiman Marcus and ordered not to look at the price tags, only at the styles of the gowns Anna

picked out for her to review. There had been an
ocean of evening wear to peruse and try on. Anna
had been highly complimentary, but extremely
choosy when it came to selecting "just the right
gown to knock his eyes out."

Greer surmised the "his" she was referring to
was Rafe and had been tempted to tell her not to
bother, but part of her had secretly hoped that by
some magic, like Cinderella, she could be transformed into a princess just for one night at the ball.

The garment Anna had finally approved, a slinky,
floor-length royal blue gown shot through with silver threads, was slit high on one thigh and, while
it had a high collar that buttoned at the back of her
neck, it boasted practically no back at all.

"One wrong move and it'll fall off," Greer had
protested, surveying herself in the dressing room's
three-way mirror.

"So don't make a wrong move," Anna had
countered, and then winked wickedly. "Besides, it
really all depends on your definition of *wrong.*"

Greer thought it best not to ask Anna to explain
that.

Shoes and a tiny purse to match had been selected before they'd made their way to an exclusive
salon where a thin-faced, slender-hipped man
named André had taken her over, body and soul,
and vowed to turn her into a goddess. She spent the

next two and a half hours being plucked, high-
lighted and sculpted.

All for this.

Standing in the guest bedroom Anna had commandeered for her, Greer stared nervously into the
mirror, amazed at the results and frightened that it
still might not be enough.

What if Rafe took one look at her and didn't like
what he saw?

Anna came up behind her, peering over her
shoulder and beaming like Pygmalion at the final
moment when his creation had life breathed into it.
She couldn't have been more pleased.

"So, what do you think of yourself?"

The person looking back at her *did* look like a
princess, Greer thought. Someone touched by
magic. Her eyes met Anna's in the mirror.

"I don't know who that is."

Anna gave her shoulders a light squeeze. "The
you that's been dying to come out, that's who."
Turning Greer around to face her, she handed her
the tiny purse. All it contained inside was a com-
pact and a lipstick. That was all there was room for.
"C'mon, let's knock 'im dead." It was getting late
and the party had been under way for nearly half
an hour. "Besides, if I don't turn up soon, Austin's
going to have the police out looking for me," she
said, referring to her husband.

Greer pressed her lips together, reluctant for the ultimate moment of reckoning.

Impulsively, Anna brushed her lips against Greer's cheek. "It'll be all right," she promised before gently trying to prod Greer out of the room.

Easy for her to say, Greer thought. Anna was naturally lovely. She didn't need an army of people working for two and a half hours to turn her into someone who was attractive. But because Anna had gone to so much trouble to make her look this way, Greer knew she had to overcome her own fears and do this. She had to walk out into that ballroom.

Squaring her shoulders, she left the shelter of the guest bedroom.

It was getting easier, Rafe noted. Easier to talk to these people he'd come to accept as his extended family. He nodded as he took a glass of white wine from the tray a passing waiter stopped to offer. Maybe it was because he was no longer worried about gaining custody of Bethany, or maybe it was because he'd been made to see that to accept help didn't mean he was weak. Sometimes you had to be strong enough to admit your weakness.

And maybe it had something to do with the woman who had brought him here and subsequently shown him by example rather than words that sometimes things were not always what they appeared at first to be, nor did events always have to turn out badly.

Sometimes they could be downright pleasant.

Rafe nodded, only half listening as he took a sip of his wine to what his brother was saying to him. He was still slightly in awe of the fact that R.J. *was* his brother. He would have missed out on that, too, if Greer had taken him at his word, given up and gone back home to Austin.

But she hadn't. She'd had the guts to take him up on what he knew now had been an insane suggestion, agreeing to be his fiancée, agreeing to compromise the principles he'd discovered were so important to her, just to help him and to bring him here.

He owed her a great deal, he mused. And he meant to pay her back the best way he knew how.

If she let him.

Not for the first time this evening, he scanned the floor with a nervousness that was completely out of character for him. Another first.

Where was she? he wondered. He would have thought she'd be here ahead of him, worrying about all the details that went into pulling this fund-raiser off. He knew without being specifically told that her hand was behind this.

Efficient, kind and feisty. A hell of a combination in a woman. That it came wrapped in a somewhat plain package didn't faze him in the slightest. It might have even pleased him if he'd bother to examine it. He'd been raised in Las Vegas and had had his fill of glitter, flash and obvious beauty. He'd take substance any day.

Substance like the kind found within a woman with the improbable name of Greer.

When he saw Anna walking in with another woman, Rafe decided that he'd been patient long enough. There was something he needed to get off his chest before he lost his nerve and backed down. Someone had mentioned that Anna was the last one to have been with Greer. He figured the woman would know where he could find her.

"Excuse me," he murmured to R.J., setting down his drink on the nearest surface before heading toward the door. "Anna," Rafe called out, maneuvering his way through the milling press of elegantly dressed bodies, "have you seen Greer?"

Turning to the sound of his voice, Greer struggled hard not to let the blush that had instantly taken hold consume her.

Breathe, Greer, breathe, she ordered herself.

"Yes, I have." An amused smile curved Anna's mouth. "And so have you, little brother." She made the observation pointedly.

Impatient, Rafe opened his mouth to protest that he wouldn't be asking her where Greer was if he had, when he saw Anna slanting a sideways glance toward the woman beside her. He was vaguely aware of his jaw dropping down.

His eyes widened in disbelief. The woman beside Anna was nothing short of gorgeous.

Greer? It couldn't be.

"Greer?" he heard himself ask hesitantly.

Greer's throat was almost completely closed. "Yes?"

He stepped back, as if that could somehow make him understand the transformation a little better. It hardly seemed possible that this was the same woman he'd been spending all this time with.

And yet...

He found his tongue again. "My God, woman, what have you done to yourself?"

Dismay fell over her like a wet towel. This had been a mistake and now she was ruining what was probably the last evening she'd spend in his company. She felt like fleeing from the room.

"You don't like it?"

"Like it?" How could she even suggest that? Hadn't she looked in a mirror? "I'm—I'm—" He ran a hand through his hair in frustration. "Hell, I don't know what I am." Shaking his head, he absorbed the vision from head to toe like some smitten schoolboy. "I didn't know you could look like this."

Maybe it was going to be all right, after all. Greer could feel the blush conquering her despite her best efforts.

"Anna did it." But as she turned to look behind her, she found that, in true fairy godmother fashion, Anna had disappeared.

Taking her hand, Rafe drew Greer's attention back to him. "Remind me to thank her."

The orchestra had begun playing and couples all around them were beginning to dance.

"We're in everyone's way." Feeling like a duck miles away from water, Greer began to back away. "Maybe we should get off the floor."

But he caught her hand, stopping her retreat. "No," he contradicted her. "Maybe we should dance."

She wanted to protest that she didn't dance. That there had never been anyone to ask her to and no reason to learn, but she couldn't seem to find the words as Rafe took her into his arms and began to move slowly to the warm, dreamy tempo that was surrounding them.

She fell into step, following his lead. Knowing she could remain like this forever if he asked her to. He was a much better dancer than she would ever have expected him to be.

He guessed at her thoughts. "Surprised?"

She began to nod, then stopped, embarrassed. "I

just didn't think cowboys did anything other than line dancing,'' she confessed.

He took no offense, knowing she meant none. ''One of the few memories I do have of my mother is her trying to teach the four of us how to dance. She said you never knew when it would come in handy and that it was a good icebreaker.''

She didn't know about breaking any ice, but dancing this close to Rafe was certainly melting her.

''Your mother was a smart lady.'' Greer leaned her cheek against his chest, fervently wishing the moment would go on forever.

''In some ways,'' he allowed. The scent of her perfume was slowly filling his senses. Making things happen. He thought of his decision. ''I can't get over the change in you.''

She lifted one shoulder, unwilling to take any of the credit. ''Anna's been very kind.''

Kindness had nothing to do with it. And Greer's modesty never failed to amaze him. ''You're not a hard person to be kind to.''

Self-conscious, Greer made no response. She saw Anna looking in her direction. There was a wide smile on the other woman's face as she danced by with her husband.

She really shouldn't allow herself to get too comfortable, Greer thought. It was far too easy to get carried away. And then what? She had to remember this was all make-believe for Rafe. Make-believe with a definite timetable.

Greer raised her head and looked up at him. "We need to talk."

"All right," he said gamely. "About what?"

"About what the judge said." When Rafe didn't look as if he knew what she was talking about, she added, "She wants to see us in six months."

There was something in her tone that made him feel uncertain. "Will that be difficult for you?"

Going to the ends of the earth for him wouldn't be difficult for her, but that wasn't what she was getting at. She was struggling not to allow herself to go down for the third time, not to drown in her feelings for him.

"No, but I was thinking that since Mrs. Maitland had her lawyer essentially buy the Prestons off, you won't really need me anymore."

His smile faded. Still dancing, his hand tightened on hers. Rafe looked at her intently. "What do you mean?"

He knew exactly what she meant, Greer thought. Why was he making her spell it out for him? "Well, you can tell the judge that we've had a falling out. That way you won't have to lie anymore."

Something made him hold her a little closer, as if he was afraid that she would slip through his hands this instant if he let her. "But wouldn't I be lying about the falling out?"

"Yes, but—" Why was he doing this? She slowed her pace. "You're beginning to confuse me."

Well-honed instincts told him he wouldn't like where this was going. "All right, what is it you'd like me to explain?"

Why was he forcing her to say this? Wasn't it enough that it was going to happen? "Why you'd want to go on with the charade when you don't have to."

His eyes held hers as he took the plunge and bared his soul to her. "Maybe because I've gotten comfortable thinking of you as my future wife. Maybe because I want to turn the charade into the real thing."

Greer stopped dancing. She stared at him a split second before she turned on her heel and hurried off the floor, plowing through the crowd to the door. She managed to get out of the ballroom and down the hall before he could reach her.

Excusing himself right and left, Rafe made his way after her.

"Greer, where the hell are you going?"

Without the crowd to impede him, Rafe caught up to her in three giant strides and spun Greer around to face him.

He wasn't prepared for the tears.

The sight of them cut through him like a dozen sharp little stilettos. Guilt that this was somehow his fault tempered Rafe's anger. He softened his voice. "Why are you crying?"

Angry at him for spoiling everything, angry at herself for ever having believed for a single moment that any of this could ever be true, she retorted, "Because you're laughing at me."

"Hey, hold on." He stopped her gruffly. "If I were laughing at someone, I'd be the first one to know. I sure as hell wouldn't be left in the dark like this." His voice softened a shade again. "I'm not laughing at anybody, least of all you." When she raised her eyes to his face, she looked as if she were wavering. "What makes you think I was laughing at you?"

Greer brushed back the tears that had stained her cheeks. "Well, why else would you say what you did?"

He still wasn't following what she was telling him. "Say what?"

Greer looked up toward the ceiling, trying to use gravity to stop the fresh supply of tears that insisted on coming. She watched as the light from the chandelier bounced against the rectangular, gilt-edged mirror that ran along half the length of the wall. "That you wanted to marry me."

"Because I want to." How difficult was that to understand? Afraid she would bolt again, he placed his hands firmly on her shoulders. "My mother taught me how to dance, she didn't teach me how to talk. Leastwise, not to say the kinds of things a woman like you would want to hear, so if I was stumbling around like a rodeo clown his first time out of the chute, I'm sorry, but I've never done this before."

She realized that she'd begun to hold her breath and made a concentrated effort to take in air. "'This'?"

Damn it, how hard did she want to make this for a man? "I've never proposed before."

Maybe not breathing was making her light-headed. "Then you're serious?"

What had he been trying to tell her? he thought in exasperation. "Sure, I'm serious."

She needed this made perfectly clear. "You want to marry me?"

"Yes."

Greer refused to allow herself to believe him. The fall from cloud nine would be much too great to survive. "Why?"

Rafe threw his hands up. "Why does anyone want to get married?" He blew out a breath, knowing what she was waiting for. "Because I love you," he fairly shouted. "Okay?"

She shook her head. "No, not okay. You don't love me, you love the dress."

Now, that had to be the dumbest thing he'd ever heard. "I'd look pretty silly in that dress."

He was twisting her words, she thought. "I mean you saw me in it and—and that made you think that I was something I'm not."

His eyes narrowed as he tried to follow her reasoning. "What are you not?"

Was he determined to rob her of her dignity completely? "Pretty."

The answer astonished him. "You really believe that?"

He didn't look as if he was having fun at her expense, yet how could she think it was anything else? She knew what she looked like. And even if she didn't, there had always been people around to point out, deliberately or otherwise, just how very plain she was.

"Don't you?"

"No." Before she could argue the point, Rafe turned her so that she could see her reflection in the mirror. "Maybe you'd better go back and get your glasses again because you're just not seeing things right. You are pretty. Very pretty."

She was more than that, but he had a feeling that getting the woman to see that she was beautiful was going to be a long, drawn-out, uphill battle. And whether or not she was wasn't the point of his proposal. What she was inside was.

Greer waved a dismissive hand at the reflection. "That's just makeup."

He wouldn't let her turn away. He wanted her to stop and really see herself. She needed to know that she was on equal footing with people in every way.

"Can't 'make up' what's not there, and as far as I can see, you didn't have any plastic surgery between yesterday afternoon and now, so that must mean it's you under the lipstick and the eye shadow. You're not an ugly duckling, woman, stop behaving like one."

She turned around to face him. "If you feel like that, why didn't you say anything before?"

He supposed that he was guilty of that. "Partially because I didn't know I felt this way, and then when I did know, I had to work up my nerve."

She was back to being confused because he couldn't possibly mean what that sounded like. "Your what?"

"You heard me. Nerve. I said I had to work up my nerve."

"You were afraid?" Even though she said it, she didn't believe it. It just seemed too impossible. Rafe Maitland hadn't struck her as a man who was afraid of anything.

His eyes held hers. He'd never felt anything was so right before. "Yes."

"Of me?"

He inclined his head. "Of getting turned down."

This just seemed too impossible. Maybe she was actually home in bed and just dreaming all this. "You actually thought I'd turn you down?"

"Woman, you *did* turn me down," he pointed out.

She grew silent for a moment. He was right, she realized, she had. Her fear of getting hurt had made her run before there was a reason to. And it seemed now that there was no reason to run at all. She looked into his eyes and saw that he was serious. That he had meant every word.

The charade had somehow, when she hadn't been looking, become real.

Greer wet her lips. "Could I have another crack at that answer?"

It was going to be all right, he thought. Despite the missteps he'd taken, it was going to be all right.

"You can have as many cracks at it as you want until I get the answer I want." He took her hands in his. "Greer, will you marry me?"

"Yes, oh yes." Tears filled her eyes. This time, she didn't bother trying to hold them back.

Touched, humbled, relieved, Rafe brushed away her tears with his thumb. "The first thing we have to do is find something I can call you besides Greer.'' He lightly touched his lips to hers, then smiled. "How about 'darlin''?''

The smile came straight from her soul. "Works for me.''

He took her into his arms. "Me, too,'' he told her, then sealed the arrangement, and the rest of their lives, with a long, sensual kiss.

Epilogue

Megan looked from one face to the other in her office and found she had difficulty in hiding both her pleasure and perhaps, a touch of smugness— just this once. Rafe and Greer had come to her to ask for her blessing.

Again.

"There's no need to ask, you already know I'm delighted about your upcoming wedding."

"Yes, but, well, we did deceive you," Greer pointed out again, feeling that perhaps Mrs. Maitland didn't understand when they'd explained everything to her just now. It did sound a little outlandish, at least for someone who'd always been so straightforward about everything.

"Did you now?" Megan's smile widened as her eyes sparkled.

"Yes," Greer said uncomfortably. She glanced at Rafe, who had held her hand throughout the confession. It made her feel a little braver about this. About everything, really. She had this feeling that there wasn't anything she couldn't do, as long as Rafe was there beside her. "About the initial engagement and even about the summer romance—"

Megan decided to put them both out of their misery. "My dear, I might have been somewhat deceived by the engagement, but trust me, as soon as you mentioned the summer romance, I realized what had to be going on." Although at the time, she wasn't sure just why Greer had agreed to the deception. "I can do my math, Greer. You couldn't have fallen for Rafe when you were sixteen, not unless you had a weakness for eleven-year-olds."

Greer flushed. She should have known Mrs. Maitland would catch on to the inconsistency. "But you never said anything…?"

"No, because I wanted you to. You had your reasons for this and I trusted your judgment enough to wait until you were ready to tell me." She looked at the two of them, thrilled at the turn of events. "I was also secretly hoping that fiction would become a reality because you did look so perfect together. And my patience seems to have paid off." She squeezed both their hands. "So yes, you have my blessing, now and always. And now perhaps you can give Anna an actual date for the wedding so that she can start getting busy. My offer for the house still stands." She remembered the message on her desk from R.J. "And by the way, Rafe, R.J tells me you've taken my suggestion about looking into buying a ranch here to heart. I will underwrite any place you choose."

Not that he wasn't grateful, but a man had to set some limits, even with family. "I won't take charity, Megan."

"Who says anything about charity?" Megan scoffed. "It'll be a loan. And the most advantageous one I have ever agreed to, seeing as how I don't want to lose the best assistant I've ever had."

Rafe blew out a breath, amazed at the generosity. There was a piece of land that had caught his eye. It would be a perfect place for him and Greer to begin their life together. "I don't know what to say."

"Just say yes," Megan told him briskly, "and we can move forward from there." She glanced at her calendar. "Now, if you two will excuse me, I have a luncheon I'm already late for."

Cheerfully kissing them both goodbye, Megan left her office and hurried down the corridor, humming. She was still humming as she walked through the electronic rear doors. She came outside just in time to see a very pregnant, very pale-looking young woman making her way toward her.

"Megan Maitland?" the woman asked, grasping her arm.

Megan immediately slipped her arm around the other woman to help support her. "Yes, but—"

"I'm your niece, Laura Maitland. I've come about the invitation." It was all the woman managed to say before her fingers went lax.

She sank to the ground in a heap.

* * * * *

*H*ugh Blake,
soon to become stepfather to
the Maitland clan, has produced three
high-performing offspring of his own. But
at the rate they're going, they're never going to
make him a grandpa!

There's *Suzanne*, a work-obsessed CEO whose Christmas spirit
could use a little topping up....

And *Thomas*, a lawyer whose ability to hold on to the woman
he loves is evaporating by the minute....

And *Diane*, a teacher so dedicated to her teenage students she
hasn't noticed she's put her own life on hold.

But there's a Christmas wake-up call in store
for the Blake siblings. Love *and* Christmas miracles
are in store for all three!

Maitland Maternity Christmas

A collection from three of Harlequin's favorite authors

Muriel Jensen
Judy Christenberry
&Tina Leonard

Look for it in November 2001.